The Pennywhistle Tree

The Pennywhistle Tree

Doris Buchanan Smith

A TRUMPET CLUB SPECIAL EDITION

Published by The Trumpet Club, Inc., a subsidiary of
Bantam Doubleday Dell Publishing Group, Inc.,
1540 Broadway, New York, New York 10036.
"A Trumpet Club Special Edition" with the portrayal
of a trumpet and two circles is a registered trademark of
Bantam Doubleday Dell Publishing Group, Inc.

ISBN 0-440-84731-1

This edition published by arrangement with
G. P. Putnam's Sons, a division of
The Putnam & Grosset Group.

Book design by Jean Weiss
Printed in the United States of America
March 1995   OPM   10 9 8 7 6 5 4 3 2 1

For Beverly

for forty-three years
of friendship.
And still counting!

The Pennywhistle Tree

Chapter

1

The corner house was vacant again.

Jonathon and his friends were draped in the enormous live oak tree that hung off the corner in his yard as they watched the most recent tenants drive off down Carr Street. Even the dog was in the tree.

"People move in and out of there faster than Paige changes boyfriends," he said.

The others laughed. Paige was Craig's thirteen-year-old sister who had a different boyfriend every week. Jonathon, Alex and Benjy wished they were old enough to be one of her boyfriends, but she just considered them twirps, like her two years younger brother.

With Jonathon's sheltie, China, running along and barking at the tires, the four of them bicycled the short distance to take a look at the house which was a twin to Jonathon's. The two-story peaked roofed Victorians with castlelike turrets stood like sentinels at each end of this block of Carr Street. Only Craig's house, a one-story Victorian with peaks but no turret, was in between. The perfect grass, flowers, paint and trimmings made it, in Craig's mother's opinion, the apple of the neighborhood eye. Her proof was staked on the small lawn: historical marker, No. 5.

Around the corner on the George Street side someone was already looking at the house. A man and a boy wandered around the yard and Jonathon, Alex, Craig and Benjy, each setting one foot to the street, stopped to look at the boy and man looking.

Alex hunched a shoulder, sneered, and under his breath he mumbled, "Little ratty kid."

"I heard that," the boy in the yard yelled and in an instant he stooped, picked up a brick and hurled it.

"Yikes!" Alex yelled, leaping off his bike as the brick smashed into the spokes. With a quick grabbing action, Jonathon caught the bike handle on the fly as Alex leaped forward into the yard. But before Alex could trounce the boy, the father caught him by the collar and shoved him back toward the street.

"You go on along," the man said.

"He threw a brick at me," Alex shrieked, scrambling for the boy in spite of being held. From the street Jonathon, Craig and Benjy hollered protests. And China, who usually stuck either to Jonathon or her own territory, was in the yard jumping and barking.

"Sanders George, get in the car," the man barked and pointed to his son. "Get that dog out of here," he said, pointing at China. "And you," he said, shoving Alex again, "go on along now. We don't want trouble."

"You give me trouble, I'll give you trouble back!" Alex snapped, but the man was backing him toward the street.

"China, come," Jonathon commanded. She came and he told her to stay. He set both bikes down and met Alex in the yard, curling a hand around the back of his neck and urging him toward his bike. "Come on, let's go."

"Shooooee," Alex said, kicking at his bent spokes and muttering all sorts of vengeance, but he joined his friends and they walked their bikes to Jonathon's yard. When they climbed back into the tree, China scrambled with them, easily running up the short, sloping part of the trunk.

"Is their last name George, or does that boy just have two names, Sanders George 'Whatever,' like I'm Jonathon Allan Douglas?"

"Who cares," Craig said as they watched the man and boy drive away. "I just hope they don't move in."

"Has anyone nice ever lived there?" Benjy asked.

"Well, have they? You know as well as anyone," Jonathon said. From this sprawling live oak tree they had kept a watch on the world since they were three. From here they listened for the parental summons and kept a wary lookout for pesky siblings or other invaders.

"Maybe this time," Benjy said.

"You wish," said Alex, leaning out of the tree to snare the rope swing which dangled from one branch. Pushing off, he swung in an arc and landed on the porch banister, pushed off from the banister and arced again, feet scrambling for the tree.

Reaching up into a small leafy thatch which grew along an enormous limb of the tree, Jonathon pulled out his pennywhistle from where he kept it wrapped in plastic. As he played light, lilting music, they all began to settle down.

After a while they split for their days' activities. Alex, Benjy and Craig had football practice at The Rec and Jonathon spent hours every day at the piano.

Later when Jonathon returned to the tree he glanced around for his friends but they were not yet in sight. Soon, high, piping music trilled out over the neighborhood. China, who had slept at his feet while he played the piano, now leaned against his knee. He blew evenly into the mouthpiece while his fingers flowed up and down the stem. The movement of his hands was different from when they crossed the piano keyboard, but this was just as satisfying. In fact, his first love in music had been the flute, which he'd begged for since he was three. His parents had given him the pennywhistle instead. Now, finally, his real flute was on order at the music store and when he started sixth grade next week he would be playing flute in the school band.

Looking up again, he saw Craig crossing the yard and Alex and Benjy coming from the side street. They must have just got back from football practice. He continued playing, for this concert was for them. They liked to listen. They'd climb right on into the tree with him but sit quietly, waiting for him to finish. They never interrupted his music.

Until now. This time they swarmed the tree and nearly elbowed Jonathon and China from their positions.

"What is that?" Alex exclaimed, almost taking Jonathon's nose off as he swung his arm to point. China barked.

Benjy, Craig and Alex nearly knocked each other out of the tree as they leaned over one another to gape. Jonathon looked, too, and there, at the other corner, pulling up to the twin house, was a rusty, topless, furniture-laden old school bus.

"Would you look at that?" Craig gritted his teeth. "They don't even let the house air out good!"

Not finished with his music, Jonathon tried to resume playing, but it was useless.

"Would you look at that?" Benjy said as people, mostly children, emerged from amidst the furniture, swarmed over the tops and climbed or were handed down.

"Would you look at that?" Jonathon lowered the pennywhistle. "It's that Sanders boy from this morning."

"No-o-o-o—." Alex's wail descended as

14

though he were falling from a cliff. All four boys peered out for confirmation and then sank back into the hub of the tree.

"At school, too?" Alex said. "We'll have him at school, too."

"Yup. He looks exactly sixth grade," Benjy said.

"No, maybe seventh," said Craig, with a note of hope in his voice.

"Maybe he's only in fifth," Alex offered.

"Yeah," said Benjy. "Anything to get him out of our school!" Fifth would put the Sanders boy in elementary school and they were all starting middle school.

"It's a big school. Maybe he won't be in our class." Just the same, Jonathon clenched a handful of China's fur tightly enough that she yelped. His long, fine summer turned sour in his gut.

"Would you look at that?" Benjy said. On the next corner everyone, down to a toddling tot, was helping to unload the topless school bus. Sanders and his father climbed all over the bus, setting things down, or handing small things to the younger ones. Hands and arms full or empty, the children ebbed and flowed from bus to porch where the mother, fat with the next baby, took pillows, dishes, lamps, and disap-

15

peared and reappeared. There seemed to be nothing in packed boxes.

"Have you ever seen anything like it?" Alex said.

"Like what?" Jonathon asked. "Like the old yellow school bus?" The cut-off top was ragged, as if it had been pried off with a giant can opener.

"Like all those kids," Alex said.

Jonathon winced. He himself would like a tumble of kids in his family, like his Aunt Kath and Uncle Thomas had.

"How many kids? Seven?" Alex sounded as though it was some sort of sin to have so many. "And Sanders the oldest? Shooooee."

The trail of kids marching back and forth to the wreck of a bus did seem endless. Sanders worked like a man, helping his father carry mattresses, dressers, tables and chairs across the yard and up the five steps to the porch and into the house. On the porch a small girl hooked her arms around the railing where pickets were missing and swung out and back. Her laughter rang through the neighborhood.

"Look. Isn't she cute?" Jonathon said.

"Cute?" Alex almost spit on the "t" of the word cute, a dry "tuh" sort of spit.

Jonathon hunched one shoulder. "I'd like brothers and sisters," he said.

16

"That's because you don't have any," Alex said.

"Yeah," said Craig.

"Well, Alex, with a sister like Vicky, I don't blame you," Benjy said. "But Paige isn't so bad."

"Tuh." Craig made the dry "tuh" spit again. "That's because you don't have her!"

"But he'd like to," Jonathon said.

"I like sisters," Benjy said. "I like my sister."

"Yeah, but you always were weird." Alex teased Benjy by ruffling his hair and Benjy ducked away.

"Your mother will have a fit about that bus," Jonathon said, to change the direction of the conversation. He had brothers and sisters, but none he could count. Since him, Mom had had three stillborn babies.

"Maybe they'll park it up between the houses," Benjy suggested.

"It would still be beside my house," Craig complained.

Jonathon didn't remind them that all their driveways were just short stubs from street to front of house, so parking between the houses was impossible. The idea of that rusty old bus-bucket between the houses, out of sight of everyone but Sanders and family and Craig's mother, tickled him.

"It is an eyesore, that's for sure," he said, concealing his mirth. "I'll bet you can see that bus from river to marsh."

With no further word said, the four, with dog trailing, slid down from the tree, parted momentarily and returned with bicycles. Alex was a good bike mechanic and had already replaced the damaged spoke.

"You stay!" Jonathon ordered China, pointing a finger in her face. She stood with tail drooping as the boys pedaled west down Carr Street toward the Altamaha River. Popping wheelies, they kept turning back to survey the visibility of the bus. In four blocks, still short of the river, the limbs of the live oaks tunneled the street enough to hide the bus.

Going back the other way, they pedaled smoothly down the street as though they had an agreement, not even looking at bus or yard or people when they passed that house.

From the yard, mid-hoist with a chest of drawers, Sanders shouted, "Get away from here. Stay away," and he shoved the dresser back into balance on the bus and ran toward them, yelling.

"It's a public street, turkey," Alex yelled as he did a quick double spin and they all scratched off, continuing east down Carr Street. They looked at each other and shook heads, acknowledging that trouble had just moved in.

"It's an incubus," Alex said. "Get it? Incubus."

Feet on ground, straddling their bikes, Jonathon, Craig and Benjy shrugged and looked blankly at one another.

"No," they said together. "We don't get it."

"You know, from the horror films. The incubus is an evil spirit that comes in the night, like a nightmare."

"I get it," Jonathon said.

"I never heard of it, but I get it," Benjy said.

"Yeah," Craig said. "That bus is a nightmare, all right."

"The golden incubus!" Alex said as they pedaled back up the street. In front of Sanders, at the corner of Carr and George, they all rared up on back tires and did spins, daring him to say anything.

He didn't. He glared, but kept moving furniture. Perhaps his father had reined him in.

"The invasion of the golden incubus," Craig said as they reached Jonathon's yard and climbed the tree in silence. They didn't look out onto the world as they usually did but huddled in, curling into the heart of the tree.

At the base, the tree roots bulged into the

street, which had been paved around them. From this side, the trunk sloped up so gradually that dogs and very young children could easily scramble up. Several feet above the ground four massive limbs separated from the trunk and formed the holding place. The limbs stretched broadly out and up until they hovered over Jonathon's house, a sentinel for the house as the house itself stood sentinel to the neighborhood.

After a while Alex reached for the rope and swung out to the porch banister and back. Jonathon reached for the pennywhistle and played melancholy music. It was a safe, protective place, this tree, their special tree.

At supper, as Jonathon dealt plates, silver and napkins around the table, the subject of the new neighbors came up.

"I'll bet May will have a fit if that school bus is left there," Dad said. May was Mrs. Petree, Craig's mother. Jonathon looked up to see if the tone of amusement in Dad's voice was also in his eyes.

"You don't really think they will leave it there, do you?" Mom said.

"I don't know where else they can put it, do you?" Dad's eyes twinkled. Jonathon sucked his mouth still and noisily chunked ice into the glasses for tea.

"Surely they just borrowed it," Mom offered, sitting, waiting. It was her day to be served.

"Oh, I don't think so," Dad said. "I've seen the same guy driving it around and about before. Mr. George, I think his name is. Haven't you seen that bus at the flea markets?"

Last name, Jonathon registered.

"Alex called it the golden incubus." Jonathon splashed tea into the glasses and set them on the table.

"Clever," Dad said, standing at the counter, spreading flat noodles on a platter and covering them with sliced coils of rolled up round-steak and tomato sauce. They did the evening meals two by two, Mom and Dad, Dad and Jonathon, Jonathon and Mom. The other meals were usually on a do-it-yourself basis.

"I don't find it amusing," Mom said. "There ought to be some sort of rules against unsightly things like that. You act like you don't even care."

"I don't," Dad said. "Rules for yard and house are for suburbia. We purposely chose a house in town to be away from that numbing sameness. Have you forgotten?"

"I thought we bought this house because we wanted a big house and I wanted to restore an old Victorian," Mom said. She was in the business of restoring old houses, including this one. She was always up to her chin in paint or paint remover, with paintbrush, hammer, or saw in hand. That was why she went to the flea markets, to search for stuff for old houses.

Dad set the platter of steak roll-ups on the table and nuzzled Mom's neck.

"Well, May will have a fit," Mom said.

"I hope she does," Jonathon said. "I hate her yard, anyway."

"Jonathon!" Mother said.

"Well, I do. I hate yards that look like the grass has been combed and the flowers have been hairsprayed. And I think it's terrible not to allow your very own children to play in their very own yard."

"I agree," Dad said, looking at Mom in a teasing way. "We're raising a boy, now. We have the rest of our lives to raise grass. And after all the buses I had to ride to schocl as a kid, I think this may be the best use for one I've ever seen."

Mom, who really did like the exactness of the Petrees' yard, blew kisses across the table to Jonathon and Dad.

"I surrender," she said, smiling.

Chapter

2

In the morning there was a plague of Georges n the yard. Sheltie at his heels, Jonathon was going out to sit in the tree with his pennywhistle for a quiet slice of day before the hubbub began, and there was the hubbub in his yard. The children of the golden incubus were clambering up the tree.

"Get out of there!" Jonathon shouted, running toward them waving the pennywhistle. Excited by the activity, China bounded ahead of him.

Instantly, the dog was in the tree among the

children, barking. Jonathon was still shouting and now Sanders was also shouting.

"Get down. Get away. Get your dog," Sanders yelled to China, to the kids, to Jonathon as he flapped a hand at the dog to keep it back.

"China, come!" Jonathon called, and at once she came. "She won't hurt you," he said. "She just barks to talk." But he was embarrassed at the commotion. He knew it was frightening to have a dog running at you, barking.

"Keep him away," Sanders shouted, protecting the kids behind him at the curb now. They'd all scrambled out of the tree. "I'll kick his teeth in if he comes near us."

Jonathon gritted his teeth and kept a grip on China's collar, thinking about kicking teeth himself. What did they think they were doing, invading his yard this way? The whole bunch of them, even the little one who could barely walk. "She won't hurt you," he said again.

"Keep him away," Sanders said fiercely, arms out, edging the children into the street behind him. "Those dogs people say won't hurt you are the very ones who bite." Then he told his siblings, "Just keep walking. He won't hurt you. I won't let him hurt you."

Rubbing China's ear, Jonathon thought, Yeah, we agree on something, just keep walk-

24

ing. As the George children stepped off the curb, China bolted. "China, come!" Jonathon shouted, but this time she did not come.

At the curb, barking, she took a stand in front of the toddler until the baby grabbed fur for balance.

"Git!" Sanders said, stomping his foot and kicking out at the dog.

"China!" Jonathon shouted, running toward her.

"Come on, George-George," Sanders said, reaching over the dog to take the baby's hand, but the dog pushed against the little one, making him stumble and sit back at the roots of the tree. Sanders walked around the dog and tugged the baby's hand, but China bullied back and forth, refusing to let either of them step off the curb.

Just as Jonathon reached them, Sanders hollered, "Help! Help!"

By the time Jonathon collared China, Dad was at the door.

"Is this your dog?" Sanders demanded, talking right past Jonathon to Dad.

"Why yes, it's our dog," Dad said, looking around, seeing Jonathon, raising an eyebrow. "What's wrong?"

"It won't let us cross the street," Sanders said.

"What?" Dad asked.

What, indeed, Jonathon thought. What was China up to, acting like this? She was a totally gentle dog. Usually she just barked for conversation. He had never known her to threaten anyone, except Alex, once, when Alex started a fight with him.

"I'm saying the dog won't let us cross the street. At least it won't let the baby cross the street."

"What do you mean?" Dad asked, looking at Sanders, then at Jonathon.

Jonathon shrugged.

"Watch," Sanders snapped, letting go of George-George's hand and saying to Jonathon, "Let him go."

Jonathon shrugged again at Dad, who shrugged back, then released China's collar.

Obviously no longer afraid of attack, Sanders stepped off the curb to join his assortment of siblings in the street. George-George spread his arms for balance, ready to step out and China moved in front of him and blocked the way. Gripping fur, the baby tried to walk around the dog, but the dog shifted position to keep the child on the curb.

Holding his arms out to Jonathon's father, Sanders said, "See?"

"Well, I'll be!" Dad said. "China, come." The gray and white sheltie looked from Dad to baby and yipped a protest. "Come!" Dad called again. Whining in reluctance, the dog gave up her post at the curb and trotted to Dad. "Well, I'll be!" Dad said again as the dog came and the children went. For the first time, Jonathon noticed that, except for Sanders and the baby, they were all girls.

"This dog has more sense than some people, wouldn't you say, Jonathon?"

"I don't know what you mean, Dad."

"Don't you know what she was doing? Think about it for a second."

"It looked like she was trying to keep the baby in the yard."

Dad nodded, and gave the dog an approving pat. "Or, more exactly, trying to keep the baby from the street."

"Ohhhh!" Jonathon said, amazed.

"As far as I know she's never seen a sheep, but she's a sheepdog just the same, and to her that baby was a sheep. She knew that baby should not be in the street, didn't you girl?" He rubbed her vigorously and she made a contented growly sound and pushed against his hand for more. "Amazing, eh?"

"Amazing," Jonathon said, looking down the

street after the Georges. The baby was toddling along behind the others, with no one even holding his hand.

Dad had already returned to the house, upstairs to his turret writing room in the castlelike curve at the corner of the house. Jonathon checked to be sure his pennywhistle was still there and retreated to his circular music room below Dad's office. He wanted music but needed something more crashing than the pennywhistle. Inside, there was no threat of Georges. He struggled with the complicated phrases of the Bach fugue Mrs. Lunderman had assigned him. The round room wrapped him, muffling the world until he was inside the music and the music was inside him and there was only him and the music and nothing else in the world.

After a while, without interrupting him, Mother blew him good-bye kisses from the door. In another while a knock at the front door jolted him up off the piano stool. Was Mother back? Had she locked herself out? He darted toward the door so Dad wouldn't be interrupted. Nonetheless, Dad's foot was already on the stairs.

"I've got it," Jonathon called quickly.

"Okay, son, thanks. I was coming so you wouldn't be interrupted."

A smile popped to Jonathon's face at the pleasure of it, the two of them not wanting the other to be interrupted. When he opened the door, he drew back with a start. A woman stood there with an inquiring look on her face and he didn't think she was selling Avon or distributing *Watchtower* for Jehovah's Witnesses.

Uh-oh, he thought when he realized it was Sanders's mother, belly bulging with the next baby. Feeling defensive about China's harassment of the toddler, he was going to say, "They were in our yard," when she spoke first.

"May I use your phone?"

"Ma'am?" he asked back. A split second before she repeated herself, he heard her words inside his head like an instant replay. Use their phone? Did she mean she wanted to come in? Into his very house? He wanted to shut the door, wanted to say, "We don't have a phone," but everyone had a phone. The Georges had lived here less than twenty-four hours and his life was already stuffed with Georges.

"Just a minute, please," he said, and he did shut the door. Hustling up the stairs he whispered, "Dad, Dad?" pausing at the open door of his office, hating to interrupt even though Dad couldn't possibly have settled back to writing in this half minute since he'd been on the stairs himself.

As if to prove it, Dad looked up with no trace of annoyance. "There's a woman at the door, I think it's Mrs. George, you know, Sanders George's mother? The mother of all those kids? At least I think that's who it is. I thought she came about China but she wants to use the phone."

"Slow down," Dad said. "Whose mother?"

As they pattered down the stairs, Jonathon explained.

With his hand already out to greet her, Dad opened the door. "I'm Dan Douglas. And you're Mrs. George, I believe? Of course you may use the phone. Yours isn't connected yet, I'm sure."

Jonathon was astonished as Dad showed her into the heart of the house, followed to turn on the hall light and ask if she needed the phone book. He retreated to the comfort of the round room and Dad joined him. They stood listening to the murmur of the woman's voice without hearing the words, Dad rubbing the glossy surface of the grand piano. They didn't hear the end of the conversation or the hang up but suddenly, she was there in the foyer, silent as a wraith.

"Much obliged, thank you," she said in a whispery voice and she sort of drifted out. Dad was halfway back up the stairs by the time Jonathon closed the door and turned, wanting to say something, wanting to talk about how ghostly she was. Even China had abandoned him and followed Dad upstairs. Shrugging, he returned to the music room and snuggled back into the cocoon of the Bach fugue. Mrs. Lunderman liked for him to practice scales and technique but just playing Bach was an exercise in technique. He was working on a difficult phrase where the little finger played F's in eighth notes while the other fingers of the same hand played sixteenth notes. Before he had it smoothed out, a commotion of scurrying and shouting ripped through his veil of solitude. He jumped to the window and looked out, incredulous, onto a circus of Georges.

Two girls dangled from the rope swing, another walked the banister, Sanders was about to kill himself on Jonathon's pogo stick and George-George was playing monster, arms out, stomping all over the yard.

Jonathon plunged back into his music but the spirit was out of it. His fingers moved methodically and the rhythm was gone. Relentlessly he continued, trying to get back into the music, frustrated at the loss, and frustrated at his frustration. Music came from the center of his bones. How could a yard full of kids destroy his pleasure so quickly? He crashed his hands all over the keyboard like Charles Ives. Fingers, fists, elbows and all.

In a split-second lull between crashes, he heard a tap on the window. He stepped to the side window and pulled back the curtain and there was Craig on the side of the porch where it circled the turret room.

"What's this?" Craig mouthed through the glass, thumbing toward the Georges.

Jonathon gritted his teeth at Craig. As if it's my fault, he thought, as if I invited them!

Craig thumbed the other way, toward the back. Jonathon nodded, ran to the foyer, and down the center hall, to the back door and out. Alex and Benjy were there, already draped in the pear tree, looking glum. Coming from the street side, Craig said, "Mamba caramba, my mother had a fit. The little one stomped on her peonies."

They reached for the tree at the same time and looked at each other. Unlike the giant oak out front, the pear tree was not broad and branchy enough for all four of them anymore.

"What's going on?" Alex asked, as Craig swung into the tree. A couple of not yet ripe pears shook off and thunked to the ground.

Jonathon, remaining below, shrugged.

"Aren't your parents having a fit?" Craig said. "They're all over your yard."

"Aren't you observant," Jonathon said. "They just came."

"We can't even get to the tree without them . . ." Benjy let the rest of the sentence hang, as heavy as the fruit plump and ripening and weighing down the limbs of the pear tree.

"We've been invaded," Alex said.

The other three looked at one another, rolling eyes. "We've had to retreat from our own territory," Craig said.

"There's your mom home," Benjy said.

"Oh yeah?" Jonathon said, turning too late to see Mom's car pass the corner, but hearing it, now, as it swung into the driveway. "Now watch," he said, happier, dusting his hands together and trotting through the inside yard between his house and Craig's. Mom would rout the Georges.

The boys scampered to the corner of the house and watched Mrs. Douglas step out of the car, tucked between azaleas and hydran-geas. She pursed her lips and stared over the blue top of her car. The laughter of the George kids shrieked around the corner from the front yard. As Jonathon peered around the corner he saw Mom wade through the Georges with hardly a glance at them. He darted in the kitchen door and ran to the hall just in time to follow her up the stairs.

"Dan? Dan? How could you allow this?" she said, plowing right into the office without knocking.

"Fran-ces," Dad said, "I'm in the middle of a difficult passage."

"Da-an," she said, imitating his tone. "I'm in the middle of a difficult homecoming. Don't tell me you don't hear that."

Dad blinked and pushed away from his desk and for the first time Jonathon understood that Dad, too, worked inside a cocoon.

"Oh, there are those kids again," he said, laughing, when he'd walked over and looked out the window. "China wouldn't let that little one off the curb." Automatically he reached down and patted the dog again. Her tail wagged at the attention and in pleasure of having everyone here together so she wouldn't have to choose who to be with.

Mother looked puzzled and Dad told the story.

"Do you think we can teach China to let them have the street but keep them out of the yard?"

"Aww, honey." Dad slid his arm around her.

Jonathon looked out the window. Sanders had not killed himself, had in fact mastered the pogo stick and was bounding up and down the sidewalk from house to street and back again.

"Will you go chase them out of the yard?" Mom said to Dad.

"Chase? That's a pretty strong word, Frances. They're just kids."

"I feel strongly about this, them swarming all over the yard like a hive of bees."

"Yeah," Jonathon said. Swarming was the word for it, although the way Mom said it made him feel they were being mean like Mrs. Petree.

Dad looked from Mother to Jonathon and back to Mother. "Well, I say he or she who wants them out of the yard is he or she who should get them out of the yard. Isn't that what you'd say?" He chucked Mother under the chin and she moved her head away from his hand. Dad returned to his desk. The shell he drew around himself was almost visible.

Chapter

3

In these lovely last days before school began, the Georges had taken over Jonathon's yard.

"I'd just tell them to leave," Alex said boldly.

"You tell them, then," Jonathon said. The four boys were in Jonathon's backyard, crowded in the pear tree among fattening fruit.

"It's not my yard," Alex said.

Is so, Jonathon wanted to say. His yard had belonged to all of them since they were three.

"I don't know what I'd say, but I'd try to think of something," Benjy said.

"Just say buzz off, you turkey," Craig said.

"Turkeys. Plural," Jonathon said.

"Oh, for the good old days in Terra City," Alex said.

"Yeah," said Craig. "When our yard was our yard."

"Hmmph," Jonathon said. At least Craig realized it was "their" yard. He longed for Terra City himself, where several years ago they had spent elaborate hours constructing and traveling through a small city which crossed his front yard from hydrangea roots to tree roots. Now they were hiding in the backyard.

"My mother called the authorities," Craig said. "What are your folks doing?"

"Trying to be kind, I guess," Jonathon said a bit feebly.

In truth, he didn't know what they were doing. These same exact conversations from the yard were taking place between his parents, about who should purge the place of Georges.

"Why don't you just tell them to go home?" Mom said, wanting Dad to do it because he was home most of the time.

"You tell them," Dad said, "since it bothers you so much."

Someone tell them, Jonathon thought, but he didn't dare spout off to his parents. Why were they having such trouble with this, he wondered. They were the adults. Mom, maybe, found it too difficult to have kids around when they weren't hers. She'd tried so hard to have more. And Dad, well, . . .

Jonathon knew he was like his father, chicken. His tender-hearted father wrote, of all things, romping, stomping action novels. And except for his own first "get away from here" outburst, he couldn't think of what to say to get rid of the Georges either.

In addition, Sanders's mother, so quiet and timid she barely cast a shadow, came almost daily to use the phone. As they had that first day, Dad and Jonathon stood huddled in the music room, feeling as displaced from their own house as Jonathon felt from the yard.

"Uh-oh," Dad said one day as they stood, hands in pockets, watching for the silent figure to reappear in the front hall. Jonathon looked at Dad to see why he'd said uh-oh.

"Uh-oh," Jonathon said, for he saw through the sidelight of glass that Mother was coming.

Mom navigated through Georges with a mild expression on her face only until she was past them. Then she looked ferocious. From the doorway of the music room, Dad held out a cautioning hand and signaled down the hall.

"Who?" Mother mouthed, moderating her expression as she followed Dad's signal.

Dad mouthed back, "Mrs. George."

"Who?" Mom mouthed again.

In a series of quick, staccato points, Dad stabbed his finger toward the window, toward the yard. Eyebrows arched nearly to her hairline, Mother confirmed the information not with staccato points but with two lengthy beats, one to the yard and one down the hall.

Silent Foot, as Jonathon silently dubbed her, reappeared right into the center of Mom's point.

"Thank you," she said in a half-heard voice. With a bob of her head she moved to the door without looking at Dad or Jonathon or acknowledging Mom's presence.

"You're certainly welcome," Dad said heartily, moving into the hall, to the door. "Glad to do it."

Mom hesitated and focused, Jonathon thought, on the roundness beneath Mrs. George's loose dress. Then she turned her back and examined the reflection of her hand in the ebony surface of the piano.

"Any time," Dad said cheerily as Mrs. George floated out. Was Mother counting beats—two, three, four, five, six—to give Dad time to close the door?

"Any time?" she said, whirling as soon as the door clicked. "What's this 'any time' business? I don't want her in my house." She pointed her finger at the window with such force Jonathon thought the power of it might pierce the glass and zap Mrs. George in the street.

"Frances, they don't have their phone in yet," Dad said.

"And they won't get one as long as they can use ours," Mother snapped.

"Oh, come on, Franny."

Jonathon could have said the next words himself before Mom said them. "Don't you Franny me."

Dad shrugged and held out his hands in defeat. At least they were even on their surrenders, Jonathon thought.

Mother stepped into the foyer and looked through the leaded glass panel and frowned. Georges were still all over the yard, Sanders bounding on the pogo stick, two girls dangling tandem from the swing, two more tottering atop the porch railing. One was methodically pulling leaves off the hydrangea bush. Mrs. George had scooped up George-George, Jonathon noted, and was carrying him away, although the baby reached back, waggling his hands, wanting to stay.

"What are they doing?" Mother asked Dad.

He shrugged his "don't know."

"Why didn't she take them home with her?"

"She took one," Dad said with a teasing smile. "That's one less than was here when she came."

"What are you saying, Dan?"

"I'm saying the children were already down here when she came to use the phone."

Pouncing on every pronoun, Mom said, "*You* mean *she* had to wade through *our* yard past *her* children to use *our* phone?"

Jonathon's eyes ping-ponged between Dad and Mom.

Dad smiled. "Yes, ma'am, Franny, that's what I'm saying. I don't know why you're so upset, Fran. We always did want more children."

Mother looked absolutely stunned.

Jonathon was stung, too. Why would Dad say that?

For a moment Mother just stared. Fishing through her purse, she seized something and clacked it onto the bookshelf near the door.

"What's that?" Dad said, moving to see.

"A quarter," Mom said. "Next time she comes, hand her this and tell her there's a pay phone at the Quik Stop."

Dad gasped and said, "Fra-anny. That's four blocks, and she's very pregnant."

Mom didn't even say "Don't Franny me" before she stalked up the stairs.

Dad followed. "Oh, Franny, I'm sorry. What a stupid thing for me to say. I don't even know why I said it. It's just that I feel sorry for those kids, for Mrs. George."

Jonathon stood frozen in the hallway as Dad's voice faded in the distance. He hadn't gone into his office but had followed Mom down the upstairs hall. Soon Jonathon heard the louder than necessary slap-slap-slap of a paintbrush. He was still standing there when Dad came back down. Without a word, Dad reached for the doorknob, opened the door and walked out.

Jonathon jumped back, oddly afraid for the Georges as well as for the feeling he might somehow be sucked out into the midst of them. He slipped into the music room, sidled up to one of the long windows and pulled back the curtain one finger width.

Dad simply sat on the stairs.

The Georges were so involved in their games they didn't even notice him at first. Then one of the little girls leaped from the banister and sat beside him.

"Are you the one who lives here?"

Jonathon shook his head. How stupid could they be? Did they think this was the public recreation center? Who did she think this was, this man sitting on the porch, if not the one who lived here? Dad nodded and the girl pointed across Craig's yard to her own house.

"What is your sister doing?" Dad asked, inclining his head toward the hydrangea leaf collector at the bottom of the stairs.

"I don't know." The girl shrugged. "Valencia, what are you doing?"

"I'm getting plates," she said. "A whole set of plates." She held out the stack of large, roundish leaves for admiration.

"I'll bet your dolls will appreciate those plates," Dad said.

"I don't have any dolls," Valencia said, shaking her head. "Every time I get one . . ." Her voice faded and her eyes darted from one to another of her older sisters, then to Sanders, then to her feet. "Every time I get one . . . it . . . it gets lost."

Just what I thought, Jonathon thought. They don't take care of their stuff and now they're down here tearing up mine. Sanders pounded back and forth on the sidewalk, away from Dad, then toward him.

"Maybe next time you can have a special

place to keep your dolls so they won't get lost," Dad said.

"The young'uns keep tearing up each other's things," Sanders said loudly. "They tear them up or lose them."

Yeah. Confirmation, Jonathon thought.

"Too bad," Dad said, cocking his head to one side. "I hope you won't tear up or lose any of our things."

"Oh, no, Mister," Sanders said. "We'll take good care of them. That rope swing is neat the way you can swing from the yard or the tree or the railing. And what's this thing called?" He bounced on the pogo stick.

"It's a pogo stick," Dad said.

"Huh?" said Sanders, so busy bouncing that he and Dad had to run "Huh?" and "pogo stick" through three repeats before Sanders said, "Oh, I got it. Pogo stick."

"We don't have anything to play with," one of the girls said.

Now Jonathon said, "Huh!" but with an exclamation point, not a question mark.

Sanders shrugged. "All our stuff gets torn up."

Jonathon was glad the pogo stick, the swing and the banister were sturdy enough to probably withstand the George attack. He wasn't too sure about the hydrangea bush. Maybe if he went through his old stuff and gave them some things, they might stay home. Mother had a room full of his old toys, saving everything for that brother or sister who never seemed to arrive safely. His mind went particularly to the plastic three-wheeler with the big front wheel. That should keep several of the girls occupied.

Jonathon's attention snapped back to the porch.

"You mean you want us to go?" Sanders was saying loudly.

Shoo! He'd missed the beginning of Dad's assault. Yea! Go get 'em, Dad, he thought.

"Well, no, I don't mean right this minute. because I'm here. What I'm saying is that it's not a good idea to play in someone's yard without permission and unless they're outside with you."

"Really?" said one of the little girls.

"Is that right? I never heard that before," Sanders said.

"We never heard that before," the girls repeated after Sanders, like echoes.

"That's right," Dad repeated.

"That's right," echoed one of the girls.

Jonathon ran his tongue around inside his lips, amazed at the attempted con job.

Sanders looked at the kids and then at Dad. "We'll go now," he said.

Behind the curtain Jonathon laughed and sighed with relief. Dad's quiet method had worked. He had really got them out of there. Jonathon looked up, wondering if Mom was observing this, but, no. She hadn't come downstairs and from upstairs she couldn't see over the porch roof. Besides, he still heard the slap of the paintbrush.

Incredibly, Dad was saying no, they didn't have to leave right now, "Because I'm here. Right now it's okay."

No, Dad, no! Jonathon thought. It's not okay!

"But I might be outside sometime when I don't want company," Dad continued.

"Like when you're washing your car?" Sanders asked. "You keep it so shiny."

Jonathon laughed again. If he had a video camera he could make a comedy out of this. The "pogo stick" and the repetitive "huhs" and now this bit about the car. The state of Dad's car was a family joke, because he shined the cars only when his writing wasn't going well. A dirty car, in other words, was good news.

"Yeah, something like that," Dad said. "Or maybe if I just want to sit here thinking."

"Are you going to stay out here with us for a while?" Sanders asked.

"About ten minutes," Dad said. "How's that?"

Jonathon opened his mouth with a silent tigerish roar. "Thanks a lot, Dad," he thought. "That's sure getting rid of them."

Chapter

4

When the music store finally called about his flute, Jonathon happened to answer the phone himself.

"Dad, Dad, it's here!" he yelled, running up the stairs, not even thinking about interruptions.

"Hey, whoa, just a minute," Dad said, knowing exactly what "it" was. Jonathon whooped and leaped and slapped his sides and ran back and forth from Dad to front door like an excited puppy. China also leaped and barked.

"We have to go get your mother," Dad said,

walking quickly down the stairs. "She won't want to be left out of this."

At the car, Jonathon happily pulled pine straw from the windshield wipers, and teased Dad back. "The writing must be going good, huh Dad?"

Everything was going good. His flute was here! The next James Galway was on his way. They stopped a few blocks away to pick up Mom from the old Victorian she was restoring. "If you don't mind me smelling of paint and mineral spirits," she said, as she put down a brush and wiped her hands.

"Heck, no!" Jonathon said. He didn't mind the smell of anything and he sure didn't want to wait for her to clean up and change clothes. Besides, she wasn't really Mom without spattered paint and hair awry.

As soon as Dad stopped at the curb, Jonathon jumped out and ran ahead of them into the store. Behind him he heard Dad greet someone. Still moving forward, Jonathon glanced back to see who Dad had spoken to. It was Sanders George, who was standing in front of the store, looking in. Full of his own excitement, the Sandersness didn't even penetrate for a moment. Then it did. The phantom of the incubus. Even here!

In the window was a display of instruments: trumpet, trombone, guitar, keyboard, drums and amplifiers. Face squashed against the glass, Sanders was staring in.

For one split second irritation rushed through Jonathon, but the clerk was already lifting the black flute case. As eager-eyed as Sanders, Jonathon pressed up to the counter. The clerk opened the case so slowly it was as if time were suspended, or as if the crown jewels were within. They were. When at last the lid was lifted, pieces of the flute gleamed silver against a plush red velvet lining.

Jonathon and Mom and Dad all three sighed in admiration.

One by one, the clerk lifted and connected the pieces until the flute was whole. Then he held it out to Jonathon's reaching hand.

Holding the silver tube to his lips, Jonathon blew softly, and even he was surprised at the quiet, mellow sound.

"Ohhhh, I seeeee!" the clerk said with appreciation. "You already know how to play."

Jonathon shrugged. "A little. I have a bamboo flute."

"Most people have trouble getting a sound out at all, much less such a golden tone."

Jonathon grinned at the compliment, at the idea of the silver flute with the golden tone. Not wanting to mess up, he kept blowing the same note while his parents finished the process of the purchase. The clerk took the flute apart and coached Jonathon in the connecting and disconnecting. At last Jonathon nestled the pieces and closed the case with a satisfying click. When he curled his fingers on the handle, it seemed fashioned just for his hand. There was no Sanders, no incubus in his world.

Then outside, halfway across the broad sidewalk and blocking their path, the apparition appeared. They could walk around it, or, Jonathon thought, walk right through it as though it wasn't there.

The stark, yearning look stopped them.

In a barely audible voice, the usually loud-mouthed Sanders whispered, "I wish I had me one."

The very atmosphere turned white, blotting out sidewalk, buildings, traffic. The earth slowed to a drag.

Through the denseness came Dad's voice, as thick and slow as the air.

"Oh, my . . . I wish you had one, too. We had to save and save for this one."

Mother put a hand to Jonathon's shoulder and nudged him on. His feet moved, but he wanted to stop and thrust the case at Sanders, saying, "Here. Take it." He had never seen such raw hunger, and he wanted to feed it. He also thought such an exquisite gift might banish this boy Sanders from his life.

Pushed along by Mother, he was soon in the car and encased in metal and glass, as though the car were his case. The flute dangled dumbly from his hand as he and Sanders locked eyes across the sidewalk. Jonathon leaned toward the window until his face was smashed into cool glass as Sanders's face had been mashed against the storefront.

Suddenly Sanders ran toward the car.

"I'm going to be in the school band, too," he shouted.

Dad pulled out and broke the connection between locked eyes.

"Well," Mother said with the recovery of breath. "Well."

Dad nodded.

"I wanted to give it to him," Jonathon whispered.

Both parents turned to glance at him.

A small rain began and splashed miniature cat tracks on the windshield.

Dad turned the wiper to "intermittent."

Swish . . . swish . . . swish

Six seconds between the swishes. Dry spots on street and sidewalk darkened with rain.

"Me, too," Dad said, stretching around to touch Jonathon. "But I'm glad you didn't."

Chapter

5

At home, Jonathon stroked the flute as he put it together. Positioning his lower lip at the edge of the hole, he blew. China cocked her head with interest. The one mellow note was so satisfying he didn't, at first, try for others. When he did, the mellowness didn't hold. He was not James Galway, but he smiled anyway. Perhaps, he thought, he could give Sanders his pennywhistle. He argued around inside himself as he blew his steady, mellow note. Yes. No. Yes. No. That hungry look, that quiet voice was as large inside him as the having of the flute. He felt he knew more about Sanders from that one moment than he knew about Craig and Alex and Benjy. More than he wanted to know about anyone.

Yes. The pennywhistle. He'd still have the bamboo flute and could easily get another pennywhistle. Maybe it would satisfy Sanders enough to keep him home, playing the pennywhistle. He nodded to himself with a mixture of good and ill will. He still wanted Sanders out of his life. But there was no way out of being in the band with Sanders George. What kind of instrument did Sanders have? Or would he have one of the school instruments, which were the large ones? Yes, a drum or tuba would suit the loud, honking Sanders. As far as he knew, the school didn't furnish flutes, so at least Sanders would not be in the flute section.

That thought was comforting enough for him to risk other notes on his own magic flute. They were feeble, but incredibly lovely, nonetheless. And while he doodledy-doodled up and down the keys, he thought about giving Sanders the pennywhistle. Alex and Craig would never understand such a gesture, but Benjy might. They'd started football at The Rec, so he'd just be sure to give the pennywhistle to Sanders when they were safely away at practice.

Now, with the thought of it, he remembered his earlier idea.

At lunch, as they each made their sandwiches, he tried it out on Dad.

"I was thinking," he said as he spread mayonnaise and layers of bologna, tomato, onion, pickles and sprouts, "that maybe I could give the Georges some of my old stuff."

"What a generous idea," Dad said, making a peanut butter and jelly.

"Uhhh." Jonathon took a huge bite of sandwich to stall, unsure whether to admit the idea was not from generosity but just to keep the Georges out of the yard. "I was thinking of, maybe, the plastic three-wheeler and the big dump truck and the Legos and the dolls."

In fact, he hadn't thought at all except just that moment, taking inventory of what he thought was in the storage room. After what Dad had said to them, the Georges took it as an invitation to come over whenever he or Dad was in the yard. For himself, he'd rather they came when he was *not* outside.

"Do you think Mom would mind?" Actually, he was changing his mind about giving the pennywhistle. It was not because he would miss it because it was such a part of himself, but that he just didn't want to give a part of himself to Sanders.

Dad licked his fingers where a blob of jelly had fallen on them. "Not the dolls. Above everything your mother treasures those dolls."

"Yeah, I guess," Jonathon said. Mom was especially saving his dolls for a daughter, even though she was proud to have got them for him, a son. Benjy was the only other boy he knew who had dolls. When they were little, Alex and Craig always wanted to play with the dolls because they weren't allowed to play with them at home.

"The three-wheeler is a good choice," Dad said. "I don't know if you want to flood them with stuff, though."

"That's exactly what I want to do, Dad." Before he could stop himself, he confessed. "Give them enough stuff so that they'll stay home."

"Ah, Jonno, I know." Dad reached over and ruffled his hair. "But put yourself in their position. If you didn't have anything, would you want it pointed out by being given too much?"

"Well," Jonathon said, thinking of Santa Claus or the good fairy, or the fabled three wishes that could get you heaps and loads of everything you ever wanted. "Yes, actually. I would."

"Now, my good man," Dad said, "what is it you would like to have that you don't have?"

Jonathon thought a minute, ready to reel off a list, and he realized he didn't have a list. The things he most treasured were his piano, his bike and, now, the flute. He was only mildly interested in computers, and he could use Dad's sometimes, which was enough. Most of the other kids were wild about computer games, but he'd rather spend the time at the piano.

"Nothing, I guess." He grinned and Dad ruffled his hair again.

"How about the three-wheeler for starters?"

"I was thinking of seven things, something for each of them."

"That feels like a flood to me. How about just the one thing? It should keep most of them occupied."

"I hope they love it as much as Sanders likes the pogo stick." Jonathon wasn't ready to give away the pogo stick. He was the only person he knew who had one. He dragged the plastic clunker out of the storage room, carrying it by the handle. It had been one of his favorite toys.

"How do we get it to them?" Jonathon asked Dad as he set the toy in the front hall near the door.

Dad laughed. "I think if you just walk out front, they will come."

Jonathon laughed, too. So, Dad knew what he had done with his sideways invitation. The two of them went out, being sure China stayed in, and put the toy on the sidewalk and sat themselves on the steps. You could have timed the Georges. A hundred and twenty seconds? Surely not longer. And here they came, every last one from Sanders George to George-George. They hit the rope swing, the pogo stick and shrieked at the appearance of something new. It was amazing how quickly and easily they shared, how they took care of one another.

"You two get on," the oldest girl said to two smaller ones. One sat and one stood on the back holding the waist of the first, while the older girl pushed them both up and down the sidewalk.

Jonathon was waiting for Dad to announce the giving until he saw that Dad was waiting for him to do it. He didn't know what to say or how to say it, but because he wanted those kids out of his yard, he spoke. "I thought you might like to have that."

Dad nodded and gave him a thumbs up.

The girls heard him, looked at him but just

continued the plastic rattle up and down his sidewalk. Jonathon looked at Sanders who was pogoing happily and seemed oblivious. Moving onto the sidewalk, Jonathon said, "I mean, you can have it to keep."

Now Sanders stopped bouncing and looked at him. "You mean it?" he said.

"To take home," Jonathon said, but Sanders didn't pick up the toy and gather up the girls to go home. Jonathon looked over his shoulder to Dad for help, but Dad was gone, nowhere in sight, probably already back upstairs clacking on the keyboard. He felt abandoned.

Hands on hips, almost shouting, he said, "I said you could have it, to keep, to take home." He even made shooing motions, but dropped his hands abruptly when he realized he was doing it.

"Really?" one of the girls said.

"You mean it's ours? To keep?"

"Yes," Jonathon said, smiling that finally they were catching on. Take it and go before I change my mind, he wanted to shout. But he didn't and they didn't. They continued their circuit of the sidewalk, making marvelous exchanges for turns, Sanders pushing George-George and one of the bigger girls almost bumping her chin with her knees.

"Did anyone hear me?" Jonathon asked loudly.

"Yes, we heard you," Sanders said. "Thanks. You can see how much they like it." Still, they didn't stop playing, taking turns, one ride up and down the sidewalk and then changing riders. They were enjoying it, but they weren't going home.

Jonathon retreated. To the house, to the piano, but he couldn't find the music in the middle of his bones and so he practiced technique instead. Three octave scales. Thumb under third finger, then under fourth finger four times going up. Middle finger over thumb, then fourth finger over four times coming down. On the left hand, the weaker, slower, lag behind left hand it was the reverse. He dropped his right hand to his lap and practiced only with the left. Mrs. Lunderman was always encouraging him to strengthen that left hand. Up and down, up and down he went, left hand only. C scales, D scales, E scales, F scales until he'd done them all and begun again and lost himself in the routine of it.

Suddenly he burst out of the trance. He was doing the left-handed scales rapidly and on automatic. He jumped up with a shout, sat back down and put the right hand on the keyboard with the left, and the left hand kept up, the left hand even leaped ahead until it was the right hand lagging.

"Wow! I did it," he shouted aloud to himself. "My left hand is faster than my right!" He leaped and shouted and ran out of the music room into the hall, across to the living room, through the dining room, into the kitchen and back into the hall and swung around the newel post. "I'm really going to do it! I'm really going to be a pianist!" With a gasp, he shut up and looked upstairs. He waited for a roar from Dad but there was no roar. He sighed with relief.

Then he heard silence from outside, too. More relief. He peeked out the panel of leaded glass. The yard was quiet and almost still. From recent children, or wind, the rope drifted in a small sway.

And, and, and . . . he put his hand on his hip in exasperation. The plastic three-wheeler was there on the sidewalk. Oh, nooo, he wailed, but quietly so as not to disturb Dad any further. Why hadn't they taken it home? Did they think he meant for them to use it here? How had that backfired? He was tempted to go out, yank it up and march down to their house and plunk it down in their yard and say, "Here, keep it, and stay home!" but he stayed where he was, staring out through the patterned glass.

Chapter

6

Before the first day of school, Mother solved he three-wheeler problem. When she heard the tory she watched for the next passing of Georges and told them clearly to take the riding oy home. Again they didn't. The next time she aw them she called to them, picked up the toy nd walked toward them, shaking it. Hesitating, Sanders returned to take it from her and, lmost reluctantly, he took it home.

Beginning school was like an escape. Even if he Georges still came in a swarm, there would e less time for Jonathon to know it. As the four of them started out he leaped and twirled for joy.

"You're acting like you're still in elementary school," Alex chided.

"Yeah, you're so old. I'm still a kid." Arms out, Jonathon turned circles until he was dizzy. He didn't feel any older going to sixth grade than he'd felt last year going to fifth. So what if it was a different, larger school, it was right there next to their old school. All the schools were on adjoining campuses.

On his last twirl, as they crossed Whitaker to George Street, he saw Sanders.

"Shooee," he said. He hadn't thought about Sanders walking to school the same way they'd always walked, though it was the most logical way. Even more logical to Sanders since he lived on the corner of Carr and George. Jonathon didn't want to be logical about Sanders.

At his "Shooee," the other three looked, and added their "shoe" and "shooee."

"Double-time it," Alex said, picking up the pace. They all did, but they could hear Sanders at their heels. Alex abruptly stopped and swept to one side, and they all did likewise. Including Sanders.

"Don't you know when you're not wanted?" Alex said.

"I can walk down any street I want. Espe-
ally this street. This street even has my
ame."

Jonathon and his friends looked at one an-
ther in surprise. They were so used to the
ame of the street, after George who was king
f England when the colony of Georgia was
ounded, they hadn't even thought of George
treet being the same name as Sanders George.

"I can walk fast, walk slow, or stop whenever
want, and you can't stop me," Sanders said.

"Oh, yeah?" Alex crossed his arms in chal-
nge.

"Oh, yeah?" Sanders answered, hands on
ips.

Nobody moved.

To break the freeze Jonathon said, "I'm going
o school." They all started off with him, Alex,
raig, Benjy. And Sanders. Before he knew
hat was happening, Sanders and Alex were
nto a hip-bumping match, which escalated to
noving, grabbing clothes, and a full-fledged
cuffle. Sanders slung Alex down and stomped
ff toward school.

All three reached to pull Alex up, but he
aved them away.

"I'm all right, I'm all right. Tuh. That buzzard
in't hurt me." Sanders was a block down the

street before Alex led them onward again. Sand
ers had not looked back.

School was different after all. Hordes of stu
dents surged in the hallways, students from a
six elementary schools in Hanover. There wer
innumerable sixth-grade homerooms and th
building sprawled out from a hub like the leg
of a spider. They followed banners to the sixth
grade wings, and a unified shout went u
when they realized that their homerooms were
at least, down the same leg of the spider. The
were not, however, in the same homeroom.
Craig and Benjy were in separate homeroom
Jonathon and Alex were with each other bu
had also drawn Sanders. And there he was, i
a back-row seat.

"Well, if it isn't George Sanders, child of Th
Yellow Incubus," Alex said loudly, crossing th
back of the room and shoving Sanders's chair
he passed.

Sanders leaped up and shoved back. "Chil
yourself. You ought to be in kindergarten."

Jonathon put a hand on each and walked b
tween. He didn't want Alex in trouble for figh
ing in the classroom the very first day of schoo
Or any day, for that matter. He found a des
toward the front, over by the windows, as f
from Sanders as he could. Alex plopped into th

seat behind him. Jonathon shook his head as though he could shake Sanders loose from this classroom.

With relief, he saw Scott Griggs beside him. He knew Scott from elementary school and he was at the band meeting last spring.

"You still going to be in the band?" he asked.

"Yup. Trombone." Scott curled a hand to his mouth as a mouthpiece and extended his right hand out and back for the slide. "You, too?"

"Flute." Jonathon smiled as he held and fingered the invisible flute. Rolling his eyes to indicate Sanders, he said, "He's going to be in the band, too."

Alex punched him in the shoulder and whispered, "Did you see who our teacher is?"

Jonathon looked up. There was an old man in the front of the room. The name Mr. Curtis was written on the chalkboard.

"Hey, all right!" They'd never had a man teacher before. He thought he'd like it, but he didn't know about such an old man, gray and balding.

The instant the bell rang, Mr. Curtis started. "As you know, there are thirty-two zillion things to do the first day of school. My policy, however, is to ignore those things for a few minutes while we talk about what is important."

Uh-oh, Jonathon thought.

"Tell me what is important to you," the man said.

There was silence until someone groaned.

"Who will start?"

"Vacation," someone called out to a whooping chorus of approval.

When there was no follow-up response, Mr. Curtis said, "Yes, vacation is important. I certainly enjoyed mine. My wife and I drove out to the west coast and up to Canada and all the way across Canada and back down the east coast. Another day we'll talk about what some of you did on vacation."

More groans.

"Band," Jonathon said. It seemed he'd been waiting forever for band.

"Band?" someone said, almost hooting.

"Yeah, band," Scott put in.

Silence again. Mr. Curtis turned to the chalkboard and Jonathon was surprised to see that his hair was dark, thick and curly in the back. "Vacation is important," the teacher said as he wrote "vacation" and "band" on the chalkboard. "And band. What else is important?"

"God is important," someone said.

"Parents."

"School?" There were hoots this time instead of whoops.

"Families."

"Spinach."

The outcry and laughter was total.

"Yuck! Spinach!" bounced around the room. A few kids gagged, which increased the laughter.

"Well," Mr. Curtis said when the mutters and sputters of "Spinach?" subsided. "I was looking for a way to bring important things to a close, and spinach does it."

It was Sanders who'd stopped them with spinach.

"Obviously, spinach is not important to most of you, though I've always liked it myself. Strength," he said, flexing muscles. "But only you know what is important for you, and what's important to you might change every day, and that's important, too. Ice cream with chocolate sauce is important." The room filled with laughter and cheering. Mr. Curtis didn't sound or act a bit old. He waved a sheaf of papers. "To some of you, your school schedules may be important. And to me it's important to get to know you." He pointed to a name chart at the side of the room. "I thought it would help me know you faster if I saw your names in front of me as well as your faces."

"Kindergarten!" Sanders protested.

"Well, yes, it might seem so," Mr. Curtis said. "But my homeroom students are always special. It does me good to see your faces as you pop up in my other classes during the day, so I want to get to know you as quickly as possible. Make sense?" He began calling the roll from the chart, looking up to identify the answering student. The names were in alphabetical order and there was no Sanders George. For a hopeful moment, Jonathon thought Sanders had come into the wrong homeroom.

But, there under the S's was George Sanders.

"Sanders George," Sanders shouted when Mr. Curtis called his name backwards. Laughter identified a few who apparently already knew how often people said Sanders's name backwards, or those who were laughing at Sanders for spinach.

"Are you George?" Mr. Curtis asked.

"George comma Sanders," Sanders said.

"Oh, I think I understand. They have it backwards."

"His name *is* backwards," Alex said. "He has his first name last and his last name first." More laughter.

"Excuse me?" Mr. Curtis said, looking at Sanders. "Please tell me your name."

Sanders folded his arms and slid down in his seat. He growled, "Sanders George. Backwards it's George comma Sanders. Frontwards it's Sanders no comma George."

From all over the room came snickers at Mr. Curtis's confusion, at Sanders George's name, and at Sanders himself.

"Names may be unusual, but that shouldn't make them laughable," Mr. Curtis said. "Mine, for instance, is Cantey so my name is unusual, too." With a smile tweaking at the corners of his mouth, he waggled a finger and said, "But please don't call me Mr. Can't, because I can."

Holding out a stack of papers he said, "Sanders, will you please help me pass out the schedules?" Sanders was, Jonathon thought, the only student whose name the teacher knew for sure. "Students, please identify yourselves when your name is called."

Sanders didn't move from his slumped position and looked as though he wasn't going to.

Mr. Curtis repeated his name.

"No, sir," Sanders said loudly.

"No, sir, what?" he asked.

"No, thank you, sir, I don't want to give out the schedules, Mr. Can't."

71

For one beat, one moment, one second, the silence was incredibly loud.

"Oh, but I can," said Mr. Cantey Curtis, scanning the room. "I can call on someone else faster than you can blink your eyes. Jonathon?"

Jonathon jumped in surprise, but the jump took him to his feet.

"Yes, sir," he said, stepping toward the teacher, reaching for the schedules, wondering, Why me?

Alternately, they read names, walking up and down the aisles handing them out. At Alex's name, Mr. Curtis said, "Alexander the Great," and Alex puffed with pleasure. Jonathon was impatient watching the others look at their schedules until the name George Sanders came up in his hand. Without calling the name he stepped toward Sanders, eyes searching the columns, and just barely able to keep a smirk off his face when he didn't see band. Sanders wasn't going to be in band, then? He almost went weak with relief. No, just a scheduling mix-up. His relief ebbed. When he'd given the last schedule, Mr. Curtis said, "Thank you, Jonathon, and here's yours," and Jonathon took it and clasped it to his stomach and didn't look until he sat down at his desk. With the utmost pleasure, then, he let his eyes fall on the page, seeking and finding that magic word, band.

Several arms were waggling in the air.

"There is no cause for panic," Mr. Curtis said. "Look at your schedule carefully. If there is a problem, please come to my desk."

Students, including Sanders, huddled around the teacher's desk while he filled out some papers. "We'll get this straightened out," he assured them. "But until we do, please just follow your schedule as it is."

Relief again. At least for today, no Sanders in band.

The bell rang and everyone flowed for the door.

"See you third period in band," Scott said.

"Yeah," said Jonathon and both boys stuck out hands for a slap, slap, hook thumbs routine.

After second period Jonathon didn't even need to consult his schedule. He moved quickly up one spider leg and down another and streamed into the bandroom with his fellow band members.

Instantly, the air seemed brighter and fresher.

Jonathon gloried in the melee and, since he knew how bands were usually arranged, he headed toward where the flutists might sit. Not knowing or caring where the trombonists would sit, Scott sat beside him, grinning as much as Jonathon was.

"I've never seen such a huge class," Scott said. Jonathon looked around, now, identifying kids he knew from Hanover Elementary. So what if Alex and Craig and Benjy weren't interested in band. All these people were! Sanders George didn't even enter his head.

"It will take the whole period just to call the roll," Scott whispered.

"I'm Ms. Millman," the band teacher said. "My lifetime ambition was to lead a band, so here I am."

She went through the process of mixed-up schedules. It had been made clear sixty-two times that they were to follow the schedule they had until any mistakes were corrected. Still, there were people here who were supposed to be in band but it wasn't on their schedules. Sanders was not one of them. Jonathon thought that brash Sanders would have come anyway, like those Ms. Millman had just called up to her desk. He looked around but did not see him in the bandroom. Jonathon was surprised to find his relief mixed up with being a little sorry for Sanders. There was only one first day.

Ms. Millman was asking three students why

they were here, if band was not on their schedules.

Jonathon was close enough to hear one student whisper, "I had to." Jonathon knew. He was pleased and delighted when Ms. Millman said, "Good. That's good."

Then she looked up at all of them. "The wonderful thing about this class is that nobody has to take it. I expect all of you to work hard because you want to, and to enjoy it and have fun as well. But, sorry," she said to the three beside her, "you will have to go to your scheduled class until you are officially changed over to band. I know you'll miss me but you'll be back in a day or two."

Their faces fell and they plodded through the maze of chairs on their way out of the bandroom. The one who'd said, "I had to," leaned down to gather her things and sat, sliding down and making herself small. Good for her, Jonathon thought, looking quickly at the band director.

Ms. Millman had her head down looking through some papers and when she looked up she busied herself choreographing their seat arrangements. She didn't notice the girl, and Jonathon didn't even have to move.

Chapter

7

By the time Jonathon returned to Mr. Curtis's class for language arts a strip of paper was taped neatly to the name chart with Sanders's name written frontwards. Sanders himself was in the class, huddled in the same back seat he'd taken in homeroom. Jonathon took his same seat, also, toward the front, by the window. This was the first time he'd encountered Sanders since homeroom.

Mr. Curtis began telling the story of the elephant child who traveled to "the great green greasy Limpopo River all set about with fever trees." The old-seeming Mr. Curtis grew younger and younger as he stretched his arms, wiggled his fingers and moved about the room. Except for occasional laughter, the students were still and quiet.

Afterwards, he talked about the importance of language, and got back to the importance of what is important. He quoted a section from a book where kids in a classroom were saying what was important. It didn't sound like what any of them had been saying in homeroom that morning until Mr. Curtis repeated what he'd said himself, "ice cream with chocolate sauce."

"So that's where you got it," Sanders said loudly. "You got it from a book. I thought you made it up."

"What a nice compliment, Sanders. Thank you. I wish I had made it up but I didn't. I only use it." The teacher held up the book. "*Stuart Little*, by E. B. White. I use many books."

"I hate books."

Jonathon glanced back in time to see Sanders fold his arms across his chest as if to close out books, Mr. Curtis, this class and school.

"Oh, no-o-o! Why would you hate books? Did you like the story about the elephant child?" When Sanders didn't answer, Mr. Curtis beckoned to the entire class. There was a chorus of yesses. "I got it from a book. A book by Mr. Rudyard Kipling who wrote lots of fascinating stories in the *Just So Stories* and *The Jungle Books* and adventures such as *Kim*. We'll be reading *Kim* this quarter."

"Who cares?" Sanders said.

"Well, I care," Mr. Curtis said with huge enthusiasm as the bell rang.

And wasn't it Jonathon's luck to have Sanders in his last-period social studies class, too? At least Scott was in this class, and again they sat next to each other. Sanders was once again called George Sanders and once again he protested.

All of a sudden having Scott next to him was not enough. There was too much Sanders in his life and as Jonathon ran it through his brain he called out, "If you didn't have your name backwards you wouldn't have this problem."

"It's better than having two first names," Sanders snapped back.

Jonathon was in double shock. He couldn't believe he had burst out that way, and he was surprised at Sanders's observation. Expecting rebuke, he looked sheepishly toward the teacher. She had her head in a book and was ignoring the exchange.

"Whew," he said to himself. Turning to Scott,

he whispered, "I never realized I had two first names."

"This year we're going to learn about the world, past and present," the teacher said. She began assigning and passing out books. "Rather than me telling you what we're going to study, let's just begin." The teacher referred them to the introduction and called on someone to start reading. Jonathon quietly sighed. To him, this was the most boring way to learn something.

To his surprise and pleasure the first part was about King Arthur and Merlin. But after three paragraphs the teacher had them skip the rest and go to Unit I, page twenty-five, to a more distant time than Merlin. The second reader began to read about the hunters and gatherers. Instead of going up and down rows, or in alphabetical order, names were called at random, and Jonathon was the fourth reader.

Sanders was called on next and thinking more of him than the hunter-gatherers, Jonathon lost his place while Sanders read about the beginning of trade and the making of weapons.

"What page are you on, Sanders?" the teacher asked.

"Page thirty-five," Sanders said.

Jonathon looked up with a blink. He'd just finished with page twenty-six. How had they got to page thirty-five? He flipped quickly to page thirty-five and it was a questions page. Questions for homework, he thought.

"We're on page twenty-seven, Sanders," the teacher said. "First paragraph. Please find the place and continue reading."

Sanders read smoothly, some stuff about the making of arrowheads and tomahawks. Jonathon looked at the picture. Merlin and arrowheads. Maybe this wouldn't be so bad.

"Sanders George, will you please find the right place. I know you'd rather have one more day of vacation, but I see no reason for us to waste a day. Page twenty-seven, first paragraph which begins, 'The survival of the group depended . . .'"

"Why do we have to study this stuff?" Sanders interrupted. "Who cares?"

"It's important for us to know about our world," the teacher said, mouth open to remark further when Sanders butted in again.

"I've heard too much already today about what's supposed to be important."

Jonathon cringed.

"Sanders, you will please remain after class. Scott Griggs, will you please continue."

Scott picked up where Jonathon had left off and it wasn't about weapons at all. It was about cooperation and survival. The picture showed the making of tools, one of which looked like an arrowhead. That Sanders was a mess.

Soon Jonathon was involved with the hunters and gatherers, their tools and their art, and he forgot Sanders as the voices droned on. He liked school in general, but he especially liked learning about people and places. He wanted to go everywhere and do everything, including one day being invited to play piano and flute everywhere.

At the end of the period Sanders did not remain after class but walked straight out the door, ignoring the teacher who called after him. Jonathon sucked breath. He didn't know where Sanders got the nerve.

On the way home with Alex, Craig and Benjy, they were all full of Sanders stories and how he'd acted up in every class. At home they went separate ways just long enough to attack their separate kitchens for snacks, then Alex reappeared out front with a football.

"Football, football, football, that's all you think about," Jonathon said, joining them with China at his heels.

"Piano, piano, piano. That's all you think about," Alex said, and he fired a pass.

Flute, pennywhistle, piano, music, music,

music, Jonathon thought as he took the ball to his chest and passed to Benjy. At least he joined them in playing sports in the street. They never joined him in music. Soon they were scrimmaging with China running and barking, trying to be part of the game. Then, quietly, there was Sanders, hanging on the curb, watching, obviously wanting to join them.

"Now what's he doing in front of my house," Craig said in a booming voice, for Sanders to hear. Sanders was, in fact, in front of his own house, Jonathon noted, but near the edge of Craig's yard. Too close for comfort. The old town lots were really small. Craig tossed the ball toward Benjy at the intersection and in two plays they moved the game around the corner out of Sanders's sight. But Sanders could move, too, and did, immediately climbing into the tree to continue his watch.

"I quit," Alex said, slamming the ball onto the pavement. China leaped at the ball but Alex caught it off the bounce and stalked off. Craig, Jonathon and Benjy looked after Alex.

"Me, too, I guess," Craig said, and followed Alex.

Benjy and Jonathon shrugged at one another and strolled into the backyard and shimmied up the pear tree. China barked, wanting to be up this tree, too, as she could be in the other.

"China, hush. Sit," Jonathon commanded. Instead of active complaining, the two boys perched in silence with words locked inside. Then, at the corner of the house, they both saw Sanders peeping. They stopped breathing, as though they could become invisible among leaves and fruit. But Sanders's eyes roved the yard, looked blank for a moment, then found them in the tree. The incubus even nodded with satisfaction.

"I'm going in," Jonathon said.

"He won't come over here," Benjy whispered, but Jonathon was already swinging down. He snapped his fingers at China and stalked through the inside yard to the kitchen door, leaving Benjy roosting in the tree like one last bird.

Jonathon settled on the piano bench with his flute first. New music, then old music. China lay at the music room window, her body pressing against the curtain. He watched her, treasuring her company, feeling abandoned by everyone else, trying to fuse himself into his music. For a beginner his fingers moved smoothly over the note holes and his tone was good. Not yet having any flute music, he played some of his pennywhistle tunes.

Soon he set the flute down on the bench and turned his hands to the piano, vaguely unsettled. He wanted to do more music than he could do on either flute or piano. Fugue 21 in Bach's "The Well-Tempered Clavier" was deliciously challenging, but the size of his hands limited what he could play in classical, baroque or modern popular music. They opened to a half-circle span, like Mrs. Lunderman's, and he worked at increasing the stretch between fingers, but his hands were still so small compared to what he wanted them to do, how far he wanted them to reach. They would grow, she kept reminding him. Separating his fingers two at a time, he turned them onto the keyboard sideways, depressing keys. When he turned his hand to playing position, the sides of the keys held the fingers, spreading them a bit farther than before.

Occasionally China shifted in her sleep, twitching a shoulder, flicking an ear. Jonathon didn't really notice. Then, suddenly he did. Something else drew his eye, and he looked quickly to the dog and back to the music, unwilling to give up his concentration.

He turned to measures 43 and 44 in the fugue. The reach wasn't great, but for two phrases the little finger of the right hand was striking F—F—F—F in eighth notes while the other fingers were playing a-b-c-d-e-d-c-e in sixteenths. The fingering was tricky, much harder than rubbing your head and patting your stomach at the same time.

Another movement. He glanced again, lost his place, then picked it up again. "A-b-c-d-e-d-c-e." As he played, his eyes kept darting at the dog and out the gap of the curtain, trying to deny what he was seeing. Sanders George was between the porch and hydrangea bushes bobbing up and down as if on the pogo stick.

Jonathon planted a Charles Ives crash in the middle of the fugue, jolted China from her sleep and bounded himself up from the piano bench. Charging to the door, he flung it open and demanded, "What are you doing?"

In a soft, almost embarrassed voice Sanders said, "Listening."

Jonathon knew it. He already knew it.

"Don't," he said and he slammed the door. Listening. Now I can't even play the piano without the Georges, he thought. He stormed up the stairs, grabbed his library card, pocketed canvas book bag and zoomed back down the stairs. On the porch he was careful not to look to see if Sanders was still lurking. But as he unlocked his bike from the railing, here came Mrs. George, to use the phone. He was surrounded by Georges.

"I need to call a cab," she said, patting her belly. "This baby is ready to come."

Jonathon threw open the door and hollered, "Dad, Dad," until Dad came to his office door. "It's Mrs. George to use the phone," he said and he bumped his bike down the stairs, stomped a pedal, and scratched off, swinging his other leg over as he rode. Around one corner and he was away. His breath steamed as he zigzagged north and west, north and west, Carr to Duke to Whitaker to King, through neighborhood side streets. He had never needed solace away from his own house and yard before. House and yard and especially the music room had always been his sanctuary. He pedaled between pines and palms, live oaks and laurels, oleanders and azaleas. When a car was coming he jumped the curb and sped up the sidewalks, then jumped the curb back to the street. At Princess he slowed down and took more care through the busier downtown blocks to the library. Only when he locked his bike to the bars of the bike rack and took the broad shallow steps to the door did his breathing slow.

Inside, Jonathon let the quiet and the smell of books surround him. He glanced left, to the children's book section, but felt pulled instead to the other side. His reading was beginning to slide over the line between children's books and adult books, and he'd gotten acquainted with some bumbling gang mysteries because of Dad's laughter while reading one. He made his way to the mystery shelves, found Donald Westlake and let his eyes and fingers trail the shelf as he decided which one to read next. It took just a moment to decide on *The Dancing Aztecs*, and another moment to check out the book and he was back outside.

On the top step, he froze. Across the parking lot by the garden was Sanders, watching. Jonathon marched down the stairs and stalked toward him.

"Why are you watching me?" he demanded.

Sanders cocked his head this way and that as though ready to give some smart-alecky answer. "You like to read?"

"Yeah, I like to read," Jonathon said, nodding toward the book bag. What was Sanders doing here, anyway, when his mother was having a baby?

"You like to read. You play the piano. You have a good house." Sanders paused. "You rich, ain't you?"

"Rich?" Jonathon jerked backwards as though he'd been hit. "We're not rich."

"You got two cars and both of them run," Sanders said. "You got a bike and a pogo stick." He glanced beyond Jonathon and eyed the bike in the bike rack. Jonathon started walking toward it, away from Sanders, glad he kept his bike chained.

"You go in there and get books whenever you want," Sanders said, following Jonathon to the bike rack.

Jonathon shivered. Had Sanders followed him before? He seemed to know everything Jonathon did.

"So can you," Jonathon said, relieved to think of something, anything to say. "You can check out books whenever you want."

Sanders shook his head. "No, I can't."

"Sure you can. Look what it says." He pointed and read the words from above the door. "Hanover Public Library."

"I ain't the public," Sanders said.

"Sure you are. Everyone's part of the public." Jonathon didn't even know how to talk to such a boy. He swung the handle of the book bag over the handle of the bike and shielded the lock while he whirled the combination.

"They'd let me get a book?"

"Sure. Just go ask. It's your library."

"Nah, they wouldn't." Sanders said. "You

think just because you have things everyone else can have them, too. I know you're rich. There's only one of you to buy food for and there's seven of us kids." Sanders thrust his chin out and glared.

And soon to be one more, Jonathon thought, clamping his teeth and glaring back. Did Sanders wish he was an only child? "Is that what this is all about?" he asked. "I've had brothers and sisters." He hadn't, of course. The stillborn babies were not real brothers and sisters, but he just wanted to shut Sanders up.

"Where are they, then?" Sanders challenged.

As he put his left foot on the pedal, ready to spurt down the ramp, Jonathon spat out just one word.

"Dead."

Chapter

8

Mother surprised them again. Having successfully forced the Georges to take the plastic three-wheeler home, she came out of the storage room one afternoon with one of the treasured dolls.

"For Valencia," she said. "Or, for all of the girls to share. I can't stand it that they don't have a doll."

"They'll just tear it up," Jonathon said, defensive for Mother. He'd been brooding about the babies since his last exchange with Sanders, and the "storage room" was really the nursery where Mother saved things for another baby who never seemed to arrive safely.

"We'll see," Mother said, stroking the doll but sounding cheerful enough.

"Are you sure?" Dad said, also watching her carefully. They'd had three dead babies, stillborn, and the last only two years ago.

"First one to see one of the little girls, give them this," Mother said, and she set the doll on the edge of the planter by the front door. It looked cute sitting there, all rosy-cheeked and smiling, in a dainty white dress.

Jonathon stood above the doll, touching its hair. He had no memory of the first stillborn baby except what they'd told him. But he remembered his odd combination of disappointment and relief over the baby girl stillborn when he was seven. Two years ago, however, he had been aching for a brother or sister. He was sure it would be a boy and they were going to name it Gregory. Because he hadn't been deeply affected before, Mom and Dad didn't think he was now. In their grief they had shut him out. They hadn't even thought to take him to the cemetery. Beside him China whined, as though she understood his memory and his sorrow.

Looking out through leaded glass, the yard was brightly warped. His bicycle rippled in the prism light. Jonathon remembered riding this same bike, alone, to the cemetery two years ago. On the way, he'd stopped to buy one long-stemmed red rose for Gregory. When he reached the cemetery he hadn't known which, among all the graves, was the right one. Reading names of the dead made him nervous, so he'd found someone to ask. He'd known they didn't have a family plot but was surprised when he located the place to discover that the baby, Greg, was the last of six babies in a small plot of which Kathleen, their previous baby, was first. He didn't even know where the other baby was but these two Douglas babies flanked the other four. He'd wished for a second rose, for her. In fact, he borrowed the one from Greg and loaned it to Kathleen for a few minutes. Then he set it, in turn, atop each of the other small graves, consumed with sadness to know that other babies died, too.

Staring through the crystal glass, he thought of Sanders and all the string of Georges, of Aunt Kath and Uncle Thomas and all the cousins. It didn't seem fair, somehow. China nuzzled his knee and he patted her head.

At the thought of Sanders, the real Sanders emerged, like a wavery mirage beyond the sparkling glass. Jonathon moved his head enough to look through the plain glass, hmmmph-ing with a bit of pleasure that Sanders was walking along the curb obviously upset about something. The face of the incubus was red and stormy. One of the little girls followed at twenty paces and Sanders turned on her, looking mean, and said something to stop her where she stood. Jonathon picked up the doll and took it out to the child.

"Here," he said. "My mother wants you to have this."

"Ohhhh!" the girl said, hugging the doll.

China ran wag-tailed around the two of them.

"For you girls to share," he added.

"Ohhhh. Okay." The girl rocked the doll. "Our baby died."

"What?" Jonathon asked, her words stark against his fresh memories. She must mean the last doll which was torn up, a doll baby.

"Mommy was getting a new baby, but it died." Clutching the doll, she turned and headed home, veering toward Craig's yard.

"Mamba caramba, stay away from my flowers," he heard Mrs. Petree yell. "You get on home."

Cringing, Jonathon wondered, what was the harm, after all? So the kid liked flowers. Wasn't that a good thing? As he returned to the house, a strange sound caught his ear. Laughing? No, crying. Was that Sanders in the tree crying in muffled sobs?

China bounded after as Jonathon rushed back into the house. The reason for Sanders's cries pulled too many of his own cords. He did not want to be reminded that babies die. The music room was too close to where Sanders was, so he scurried upstairs to his room. Dad's computer clackety-clacked behind the closed office door, and Mother, in the upstairs room that currently served as the workshop, was sawing trim for toe molding.

For comfort, Jonathon picked up the bamboo flute but wished to be in the tree with his pennywhistle. For the moment, however, Sanders had the tree. Lying on his bed he played melancholy music.

In a while, and almost without conscious thought, Jonathon drifted back to the stairs, and down, playing as he went. Hoping both to find Sanders in the tree and gone, he went out, still playing. When he got to the tree he saw Sanders was still there. He stopped playing but climbed on up, China scampering up as well.

"Don't stop playing," Sanders said. "I like it. I want to hear it. I like listening."

Yes, Jonathon thought, listening and watching. He put the flute back to his mouth, and his fingers, which had never left the keyholes, resumed moving up and down. He played his best, played to soothe himself and to soothe and impress Sanders.

Sanders, showing no signs of crying, watched wide-eyed and slack-jawed in appreciation.

After a bit Jonathon reached up and withdrew the pennywhistle from its place and its plastic wrap. "Here." He held the tin whistle out to Sanders. "You can play the pennywhistle."

Sanders reached tentatively, wanting the pennywhistle but not sure of Jonathon.

"You hold your fingers like this." Jonathon demonstrated and handed the whistle over.

Sanders placed his hands and put the whistle to his lips and blew, moving his fingers awkwardly. "Twiddley-twee, twee, twiddley-twee," he played, and grinned. Then, softly, he played "Twinkle Twinkle Little Star" sweetly and almost flawlessly. Because he was intently blowing, there was no smile on his mouth, but there was a marvelous light in his eyes.

Twinkle twinkle Sanders's eyes, Jonathon thought.

In a moment Sanders changed tunes and played the Wrigley's Spearmint "Double Your Pleasure" song, as if he'd always known it.

Then he zipped up and down down the C scale.

Now Jonathon sat with his eyes wide and his jaw slack.

"You've played before," he said.

"No, I never."

"How come you're not in band?"

Sanders looked discouraged. "We can't afford an instrument."

"But the school furnishes some instruments," Jonathon said.

"I, uh. I can't have an instrument at home. The young'uns would only tear it up." China pushed her head into Sanders's hand and he rubbed her.

How terrible if Sanders's parents really did not make sure the kids had safe places to keep things, dolls, toys, band instruments. Maybe it was good to be an only child, after all. Certainly Alex and Craig and kids at school complained constantly about their brothers and sisters. Only Benjy didn't complain.

"I want you to have it," Jonathon said, nodding toward the pennywhistle still curled in Sanders's hand.

Sanders shook his head. "You really shouldn't have given that doll to Valencia. It'll only get torn up." He offered the pennywhistle back to Jonathon. "I can't take it."

"Sure, take it." Jonathon wondered if this was the giving too much Dad talked about when Jonathon wanted to flood the George kids with toys. Or was Sanders really afraid the pennywhistle would get destroyed? It was painful, thinking of someone like Sanders with no music to play.

"Please?"

"Could I keep it here?" Sanders looked hopeful. "Can I sit in the tree and play?"

Jonathan's heart thudded. How had his sweet-feeling generosity so suddenly turned into a trap? He sucked a deep breath and puffed it out slowly. Could he say no to such a simple request? If he said no, Sanders might say that part of the tree was county property anyway, the way it hung over the curb into the street. If he said yes, he'd be giving away his freedom. Sanders would be in the tree constantly, playing twiddley-twee, twiddley-twee.

"I can't take it home," Sanders said.

By now Jonathan knew the next line.

"The young'uns would tear it up."

Jonathon certainly didn't want the pennywhistle torn up. He understood the "I can't take it home." Sanders wanted to leave it here, as he had tried so hard to leave the three-wheeler here. He wished, now, he had the silly toy back. They didn't seem to be playing with it, but he hadn't really looked, or listened for the plastic clattering. Maybe it was already torn up. He wished he'd never offered the pennywhistle and he was sorry he'd given the doll.

Letting his words out with controlled air, he said, "Sure. You can leave it here. I'll show you a good place." Reaching up along the fat limb, he showed Sanders the scruffy growth of small twigs. "A cat we used to have snuggled up here." He showed Sanders the plastic bag. "To protect it against the weather."

"What happened to it? The cat?"

"Got hit by a car." Jonathon pulled the sprouts back to show Sanders how the whistle could also snuggle there. "Look," he said, drawing out several small curved bones. "Mice, I guess. I guess the cat caught mice and ate them up here."

Sanders shivered at the little deaths.

Jonathon winced himself at the idea that life—the mice, the cat, the babies—was so fragile. He was glad he'd given Sanders the pennywhistle, even if he did take over the tree.

That same afternoon Jonathon's hands snagged and fired passes as easily as they moved up and down the piano keyboard. The game had shifted to the side street near Alex's. Nothing was said about the shift in play places, but it was understood that they wanted to be out of sight of Sanders's eyes. Amidst the tossing and catching, though, Jonathon heard the unmistakable sound of pennywhistle. He whooped and hollered with the excitement of their game, hoping the others wouldn't hear the piping music. But Alex, Benjy and Craig all three looked at him and each other with raised eyebrows.

"Another pennywhistle in the neighborhood." Benjy cocked his head with interest.

Action Alex immediately moved toward the sound with Craig and Benjy trailing behind. Jonathon stayed back. Pinpointing the sound, Alex looked into the tree.

"Sanders! It's Sanders. In the tree. He has your pennywhistle." Alex whirled toward his friends, then back toward the tree as Craig and Benjy ran forward to investigate.

Benjy hissed back to Jonathon, "It is Sanders. Sitting in the tree, playing your pennywhistle."

Jonathon eased toward the back corner of his house. If they found out he'd given Sanders the pennywhistle, they wouldn't like him any more than they liked Sanders.

"Sanders stole your pennywhistle," Craig shouted, and he and Alex ran at the tree.

"You get down from there," they both shouted, scrambling up, trying to wrench the pennywhistle from Sanders, and Sanders from the tree.

"He gave it to me!" Sanders howled, holding the pennywhistle back and out of their reach, leaning into the tree as though he were the tree.

Jonathon disappeared behind the shrubbery at the corner of the house, and China ran back and forth, barking, enjoying the fun.

"Yeah, I really believe that, you scudsy scum," Alex yelled.

"Jonathon would never give his pennywhistle," Craig shouted.

"Especially to you." Alex pulled at Sanders's shoulders, arms, ankles and failed to dislodge the boy.

"He gave it to me," Sanders screamed. "Tell them, Jonathon."

Benjy stood near the tree watching the spot where Jonathon was peering through the bushes. The dog ran into and out of the tree, barking, running to Benjy, running to Jonathon, then back to the tree.

Still leaning hard against the tree, still holding the whistle back and away, Sanders kicked out in a series of hard kicks, kick-kick-kick-kick-kick faster than it seemed anyone could kick. Trying to grab and dodge at the same time, Alex and Craig bumped each other out of the tree, down the shallow side into the street.

"Traitor, traitor," Sanders shouted as he leaped from the high side. Pennywhistle swinging in his hand and China at his heels, he ran away from them but not toward home.

"What gall to sit in our tree with Jonathon's pennywhistle," Alex said, as Sanders dwindled in the distance. China turned and loped back, sorry that the commotion was over.

"He's seen Jonathon up there playing the pennywhistle and he thinks it's the pennywhistle tree," Craig said.

Jonathon sidled up as though he'd been there all along.

"How did he find the pennywhistle, anyway, except by messing around in our tree?" Alex asked.

"Oh, his father probably got it from a flea market. We've seen him there," Craig said.

Jonathon nodded at the probability. Like his own mother, Craig's mother haunted estate sales, antiques shops, junk shops, flea markets, yard sales and even curbside throwaways for Victorian sorts of things for the house.

"But it was Jonathon's pennywhistle," Benjy said, eyeing Jonathon. "I've seen that pennywhistle all my life. I know every scratch on it."

"Well, a lot of help you were in trying to get it back, o brave one," Alex said, climbing back into the tree. "You, too," he said to Jonathon.

"Where in the world would he get your pennywhistle? He really is a thief." Craig scrambled up the tree, too, with Benjy and China behind.

Jonathon remained at the roots, on the curb. None of their words were said with challenge or accusation, but he felt challenged, accused and terribly guilty. There was no way he could think of to make this right with both Sanders and his friends. But how could he let Sanders be accused?

With a sigh, he confessed, "I gave it to him," adding a whole tumble of words about Sanders's love of music and the baby dying.

All they heard were the first words.

In a wild duet Alex and Craig howled, "You gave it to him?"

"Now every time we want to play in the tree we're going to have Sanders in here playing the pennywhistle," Alex shouted.

"And it'll be your fault." Craig spat out the "t" sound on fault.

Again Jonathon said the words about Sanders and music and the baby, but they hooted and showered him with outrage. All at once it was their tree and their friendship and there they were together in the tree, with him alone below.

"Traitor!" Alex and Craig said, slinging the words like arrows.

He felt like a traitor. To them, to Sanders and to himself. Leaving them all there, he summoned China from the tree and took her in.

Chapter

9

Jonathon curled up on the sofa and read his Westlake book. There were so many characters and so much happening he had to concentrate to keep track. It was a nice way to erase the world.

Still, it nagged from behind his eyes. He didn't know how to figure this out. Should he have to give up his old friends in order to be kind to someone they didn't like? Did being nice to Sanders have to mean Sanders had to be his friend for life?

He submerged and emerged from the book until Mother called him.

"Come on, Jonno. It's our kitchen. It's salad night."

He set the book down and plodded to the kitchen and slung the plates and silverware onto the table.

"Uh-oh, what's wrong with you?" The knife clicked against the cutting board as she chopped vegetables.

"Oh," he said as he snatched the salad dressings from the door rack of the refrigerator. He sighed, and hated himself for it. He seemed to be huffing sighs a lot lately. "It's the Georges." Why had he said Georges, plural, when it was only Sanders? Sanders and Alex and Benjy and Craig. And Jonathon. Why would he even bring this up to Mother when she had finally quit fussing about the Georges and even given them a doll?

"What now?" Mother said. She set the huge bowl of salad on the table and he added a plateful of crackers.

As he filled the iced tea glasses and tried to explain, Dad stepped into the doorway and leaned on the door frame. Jonathon left out the part where he hadn't immediately admitted having given Sanders the pennywhistle.

"Oh, sweetie." Dad gave him a careful hug as he passed from counter to table with all three glasses of tea. "Getting along with people is one of the hardest things we have to do. They misunderstand us and we misunderstand them." Dad walked over and put his arms around Mother who was standing at the table. He hugged her, then while he had his hands in front of her he snared a piece of tomato from the salad bowl. "You've certainly heard your mother and I have misunderstandings," he said as they all sat.

"Maybe they're scared you won't be their friend anymore if you're friends with Sanders," Mom said.

"I'm not friends with Sanders," Jonathon protested. "I just gave him my pennywhistle."

"Well, don't ever be sorry for being generous," Dad said.

"Sometimes it helps to ask yourself who owns the problem," Mom said.

"We all own it," he said. He'd heard her say that before so he knew what she meant. "Me, Sanders, Alex, Craig and Benjy."

"Sometimes you have to be the one to try to solve it," Mom said.

He didn't want to be the one to try to solve

it. What he wanted was to project himself to the year 2015 when, surely, it wouldn't matter anymore.

Instead, he cleared the table and went to the music room and pieced together the cool, silver flute. They had their band music now, but it was too simple beginning band music. Baby music to him. Nevertheless he practiced it a few times. How stupid it would be for him to make a careless bobble in easy music. He had looked forward to band so much and now it was hard not to be bored. He was holding himself back because he didn't like feeling like a hot shot.

Not until he turned to the Bach did the room wrap around him. The fugue improved with every repetition. Repetition was becoming memory. He was learning it. The sun bounded off a prism on the window ledge and scattered rainbows across the room. Some things, at least, were right with the world.

His immersion was successful until he heard his friends on the side street. Tiptoeing through rainbows, he nudged the curtain aside for a look. There they were, Alex, Benjy and Craig, clustered in the street beside his house, not looking as though they had any intention to signal him to come out. Go in front of your own houses, he thought, flooded with memories of so many good times. All of them, one summer, scratched Terra City into the dirt and grass of his front yard and were whoever they wanted to be in that city. As he smiled at the memory, they saw him at the window, smiling. Did they think he was smiling at them, wanting to come join them? Only Benjy smiled back, and waved. Craig and Alex just looked grim.

Okay, Jonno, he said to himself. Don't be a fool. Don't be stubborn. Who owns the problem? He really did want to go out, to be with them, have this awkwardness disappear. But he wanted them to come to him and say it was okay, that they understood. Obviously, they weren't going to. With a casual sort of stroll, and China beside him, he wandered out and joined them.

"Hi, Jonno," Benjy said. Alex and Craig didn't even greet him, but kicked at the street and watched their feet as though feet were of great interest.

Jonathon was so tempted to say, "Tuh," and walk straight away. But Benjy was there and he had waved, then spoken, and he'd already walked off from Benjy once, leaving him in the pear tree. Of all people, he shouldn't turn his back on Benjy.

"Hi," he said to Benjy, to them all, and the

word hung lonesome in the air so long that he was compelled to fill the space. "Want to have a swing contest?" he said, forcing air through his throat and moving lips and tongue. Sometimes they vied to see who could climb the rope swing the fastest, or leap the farthest, or do flips as they leaped.

Shrugs. More kicking. He guessed no one had heart or energy for rope-swing contests.

Suddenly Alex said, "Why not?" and walked off toward Jonathon's front yard, and the rest of them followed. Alex walked past the swing, however, and plunked onto the ground on the farside of the yard, nearest Craig's. They all sat or squatted low beside the azalea hedge, shielded from view of the next corner.

"What are we going to do about it?" Alex said. The evening sun angled across and speckled them with tree-filtered light. Alex broke off a blade of grass and twined it around a finger.

What did Alex mean by "it"? Jonathon wondered. The rift between them? Sanders George in particular? Or him giving Sanders the penny-whistle?

"About what?" he asked.

"You're a comedian, Jonathon," Craig said.

Jonathon rolled to his side and pulled at tufts of grass, collecting shreds in his hand as the

George girl had collected hydrangea leaves.
China lay down beside him and wiggled up
close as he snatched the yard bald in a snaky
pattern and dusted the path with his fingertips.

"Wellll," Craig said, pulling up a snippet of
grass himself. Since "wellll" meant nothing,
they all laughed.

"Rope-swing tricks or Terra City?" Benjy said,
plucking grass and clearing a path. "Are all the
cars still under the porch?"

Instantly Alex scurried up behind the hydran
geas next to the porch and shimmied loose a
panel of lattice.

"Look!" he said, bringing forth a small square
box they hadn't seen or thought of for three
years.

"Where's my Mercedes?" Benjy dived a hand
into the box.

"I've got it," Alex said, showing he had laid
claim and taken first choice.

"But I always use the Mercedes," Benjy said
as though they had played cars yesterday.

Alex was already rolling the red Mercedes
convertible onto the sandy road Jonathon had
absently created. In point of fact it was Craig's
Mercedes, but they'd seldom pronounced own
ership with this fleet of vehicles they'd pooled

when they first built the city. The fleet had been idle since that last free summer before third grade, before they had been captured by little league sports or in Jonathon's case by more intense dedication to music.

"I'm going to be the fire chief, so I need a red car," Alex announced, closing the red Mercedes in one hand while with the other he cleared space for the fire station.

Benjy lifted the "official" fire chief's car out of the box and held it up. It was red with an insignia on the door. "Who ever heard of a fire chief with a Mercedes?"

"You just heard of it," Alex said.

Benjy dropped the chief's car back into the box with a clunk, and took out a pickup truck.

With many-fingered bulldozers they reclaimed the yard for Terra City. Thatches of grass disappeared as small roads crossed the yard and wound among or tunneled under roots of dogwood, hydrangea and azalea. China walked around like Gulliver-dog until Jonathon took her to the sidewalk and told her to sit and stay.

"Who's running the service station?" he asked when there were enough roads to start the fleet rolling in earnest. "I need gas."

"I'm the fire chief," Alex said, pulling the two fire engines out of the box and rolling them into the station.

"I'm a doctor," Craig said, driving a blue convertible into a spot he declared as the hospital parking lot.

"I'm a lawyer," Benjy said, claiming a space for his law office.

"And I'm the Indian chief," Jonathon said. "And I need gas." Raising eyebrows, pursing lips, they looked at one another. As eight-year-olds they had all clamored to run the service station, arguing about it, having to draw straws and take turns.

"I'll run it myself," Jonathon said, talking to himself as he made the motions of filling his car with gas.

"What about my windshield?" he asked himself. "And how about checking my oil and my tires? Don't you give service anymore? I've changed to self-service," he told himself. "After this, pump your own gas."

In a few minutes Alex said, "Hey, I'm not going to be the fire chief. I'm going to be a stockbroker." He wheeled the red Mercedes out of the fire station and picked a spot near Benjy's law office.

"Then what am I doing here?" Jonathon said,

closing down the service station. "I'm a musi-cian and I'm doing concerts all over the coun-try." Driving his car into the car lot, he then pretended to take a plane and fly around the yard.

"Aw, Jonathon, you'll probably move to New York," Craig said.

"That's what he's really going to do some-day," Benjy said. "Fly off and leave us here in Hanover."

"He's not leaving me," Alex said. "I'm going to New York, too. I'm going to be a stockbroker on Wall Street. I'm going to be rich."

"Yeah, sure," Craig said, as Alex, too, took to the air.

"Let's don't talk about it," Benjy said. "I hate the idea of growing up. It used to be fun talking about growing up because it wasn't real. Now I can see it coming, and I hate it. I like being a kid."

"You think you'll be six now and forever and ever," Jonathon said, paraphrasing a line from an A. A. Milne poem.

Traffic had stopped in Terra City. The musi-cian and the stockbroker came only to visit and the doctor was staying at the hospital and the lawyer had his head in law books.

Without the benefit of the blue convertible,

Craig scooted across the yard in a sitting position, bumping himself across Terra City to where his yard and Jonathon's met. Keeping low, he reached out and plucked one of his mother's untouchable flowers.

"Craig!" Jonathon said as he flew over.

With the same sitting-scoot Craig returned to Terra City.

"This game is dead," he announced as he scooped up some dirt and mounded it into piles, then patted them into shapes like loaves of bread. "It died three years ago." He stuck the stem of the flower into one of the mounds.

The other three watched in surprised silence.

Alex broke the silence by racing the red Mercedes down the sand roads again, with loud vroom-vrooms, and sounds like squealing tires as he turned into the fire station. "I'm the fire chief again," he said. "Being an imaginary stockbroker is bor-ing." Taking a firetruck in each hand he screamed sirens and raced back to the stockbroker's old office which he said was burning.

"We are the only boys in sixth grade who play like this," Craig said, standing above the cemetery.

Alex reached for the fire chief's red Mercedes, and raced it along the same roads to the fire "We are the only boys who ever played like this," he said, using pretend hoses on the pretend fire and then turning the hoses on his friends for a pretend dousing.

"Our fathers did," Jonathan said, remembering that when they built the first Terra City all of the fathers came to see and talked about having done the same thing when they were boys.

"Even in second grade everyone thought we were weird," Craig said.

"Well, we are, aren't we?" Alex said. "Come on. All of you be firemen and help me with this fire. The flames are leaping through the roof."

But in the dusk, no flames leaped, either in reality or in anyone's imagination but Alex's. When there were no volunteers, Alex looked from one to the other of his friends. He stood and slowly swung his left foot and made a hard, stubbing swipe at the cemetery.

"Alex!" the others cried in chorus. Even Craig.

"Craig is right," Alex said, slowly, deliberately, stubbing again, grinding the flower and scattering the pinkish-orange petals. "The city is burning," he said, continuing to swing his foot. "Fire equipment comes from nearby towns, but it is too late to save the city." With hard blows of his shoe, left foot only, he methodically scuffed out the streets of Terra City. China leaped up, barking, and ran about adding to the destruction, which became total as Alex's foot rasped the ground. They were all as exhausted as if they really had fought fire.

As they stood in the growing dark, China was quiet and the first parental calls floated out into the night air.

Alex said, "Who cares, anyway?"

Chapter

10

The next week the four of them walked to and from school stiffly, sometimes together and sometimes with only one other and, even, sometimes alone.

"I have to go early to see the coach," Alex said.

"I have to stay after for band practice," Jonathon said.

The only thing Sanders said to Jonathon was, "Fink." He did not appear in the tree and Jonathon wondered what he had done with the pennywhistle.

Saturday was the annual Wellness Walk which they'd done together since they were six, with Jonathon's parents taking them. And without saying a word about it, there they were, Saturday morning, Craig, Benjy, Alex, waiting for the ride to the starting point at The Rec Center. The walk was ten miles and they'd managed half of it the first time and increased it to the entire distance by the time they were eight. They never added another mile to it by walking to the starting point at The Rec Center. In the car it was the same as always, all four squashed in back, exchanging banter with Mom and Dad.

At the starting line, however, registered and with numbers on their backs, Jonathon noticed they chattered with other people instead of each other.

As every year, a Marine unit from Parris Island was there to participate. Starting out by bringing up the rear, they ended up near the front with only a few energetic kids and the serious adult runners ahead of them at the finish.

At the start signal, Alex said, "Let's keep up with the Marines."

"Go for it," Dad said, he and Mom stepping out while the boys waited to follow the Marines.

When the double-timing unit crossed the starting line the boys linked arms and scurried out behind, happily threading through the crowd which parted to make way for the Marines. The hundreds of walking and running feet were like thunder. Hordes of kids hung in with the Marines but Jonathon, Alex, Craig and Benjy were in the throng as a separate, bonded unit, like the Marines. Even when they dropped arms, to better keep the pace, they held rank, grinning, double-timing, all four as one.

"Well this isn't so hard," Craig said.

"Just wait," Benjy said. "We haven't even gone a half mile yet." All along the way there were mile markers and tables full of cups of juice for the walkers and runners as volunteers marked off the numbers of those passing the checkpoint.

"Whew!" Craig said before they reached the first mile marker.

"Whew is right," Benjy agreed, but they kept pace and after a while they were in the rhythm of it, so it wasn't as hard.

"Shooe, let's get ahead of them." Alex picked up speed and began to pass and this time the others didn't follow. He gained three ranks and he couldn't seem to make any further headway. Slowing to a walk, he bent over for the few seconds it took for Jonathon, Craig and Benjy to catch up, said, "Whew," himself and fell in with them again. Jonathon wanted to laugh but he couldn't spare the breath.

At every mile station they grabbed the small cup of juice and chugged it down in rhythm with the pace, without breaking stride. From experience, even when they were merely walking, they had learned that keeping the pace was easier than stopping and trying to regain it. The Marines even spurned the juice.

Somewhere along the way Scott Griggs, from school, from band, joined them. By the seven-mile table there was only a sprinkle of people ahead of the Marines and a small cloud of kids hustling to keep up, with quite a gap before the next clump of walkers. Suddenly, there was Sanders among them as they grabbed their juice.

"Fink!" he said to Jonathon.

Scott grinned quizzically at Jonathon. Where had Sanders come from? He was an expert in just popping up. Surely he couldn't have been ahead of them and just now be dropping back. Sanders spilled his juice and smirked as he fell in step, just behind them, pounding, chanting with the Marines.

"Sound off, one, two. Sound off, three, four. What's the count? three, four. One, two—three-four."

Jonathon guessed that Sanders hadn't been in the walk at all, but had just joined in at this point. Still, his hair was matted with sweat and when Jonathon dropped back a step or two to see, there was a number on the back of his T-shirt. He wanted to flick off this nightmare, day-mare, this incubus of a Sanders sticking to him like a shadow.

"I refuse," Alex said, puffing. "Let's drop back. How about it?" On command Craig, Benjy, Jonathon and even Scott dropped back with Alex. Slackening their pace only slightly, the Marines increased the distance in an instant.

"Mamba caramba, I refuse, too," Jonathon said. Picking up his pace, he left his friends, steamed past Sanders and, powered by anger, began passing Marines. Scott kept up with him. When he reached the third to last rank, as Alex had recently done, he kept churning. He was angry with Alex for being so mean-spirited about Sanders, with Sanders for being a leech and with himself for being such a coward and shrinking behind the shrubbery instead of just admitting he had given the pennywhistle to Sanders. Besides, having worked so hard to stick with the Marines, he didn't want to drop behind now. Did they all just automatically follow Alex? No. Benjy didn't. Benjy came with him to the pear tree the day Alex and Craig stalked off because Sanders was watching them play football. And Benjy hadn't really joined in the meanness to Sanders on the day of the pennywhistle. But where was Benjy now? Back there with Alex. As his feet pounded rhythmically, he smiled at Scott. Scott was the only one he wasn't mad at.

Before Jonathon passed the eight-mile table, he and Scott overtook the Marines and were in front of them. Just barely. The pounding feet thundered at their heels and the chanting voices nipped at their shoulders. Scott moved to the side to keep from being run over but Jonathon, knees and elbows pumping, increased his speed a bit more so it didn't feel like the Marines were after him like the hounds of hell.

Another half mile and he was able to settle into the previous pace, as when he'd been following the Marines. After his extreme effort, it was like going slow. Scott put on a spurt and caught him again. They shook their arms and flexed their shoulders to loosen up. Only then did Jonathon realize that the incubus was right there with them too.

"Shoe!" he said out loud. Sanders was like static cling. He was a total parasite, a bloodsucking vampire. Jonathon cut his eyes at Sanders, who was running, staring, grinning.

Grinning? Jonathon puzzled over that a moment. Sanders hadn't yet said, "Fink!" Suddenly it was as though Sanders was made of crystal and Jonathon saw inside the wanting, hurting, needing boy. He glanced at Scott. Sanders was just a boy, like himself, like Scott. His footsteps pounded up through his ankles, shins, thighs and into his gut as though he himself was the wanting, hurting, needing boy.

"One, two, three, four. One, two—three-four," the Marines boomed behind him. Jonathon stretched out his arm with his hand palm up and, without hesitation, Sanders slapped it with a satisfying pop. Scott held out a hand and the three of them smacked hands.

From behind there was the sound of hand slapping. Jonathon, Sanders and Scott looked back. The Marines were smiling and hand slapping, too, adding extra punctuation to the thundering feet and the cadence count. In between slaps they gave the boys a platoonful of thumbs up.

At the end of the run, still ahead of the Marines, Jonathon held back half a pace for Sanders to cross the finish line ahead of him. When he found out the three of them were fifteenth, sixteenth and seventeenth and prizes were given through fifteen, qualms soured his stomach. He'd just let Sanders get the last of the prizes. Sanders whooped, and Jonathon masked his feeling as he and Scott clapped Sanders's back in congratulations. When they found out the prize was a cylinder of tokens for the video game parlor at the mall, Sanders whooped again. Scott said, "Wow!" With genuine enthusiasm Jonathon slapped Sanders's back again. He knew he was a weird kid not to be interested in the video games at all.

"You going home now?" Sanders asked, ready to walk along with them.

His feelings were swirling again. Running en masse with Sanders was one thing, but walking home with him, one on one, was something else.

"I go that way," Scott said, pointing toward Queen Street.

"I'm going to wait for my folks," Jonathon said.

In spite of having come in fifteenth and won a prize, Sanders was visibly disappointed.

"Your folks are really back there?" Sanders asked, pointing at the throngs heading their way.

"Sure." Jonathon grinned.

"Oh, okay," Sanders said. "See you."

Jonathon winced as Sanders walked off, looking lonely.

Scott headed off, too, and Jonathon was lonely himself, standing there in the crowd, finishers streaming in. He turned to watch Alex, Craig and Benjy come across the finish line, still among the early finishers but way behind the Marines. Gasping for breath, they laughed and slapped backs and hands, reaching out for Jonathon in the old comradely fashion. Then they slung arms around one another, those three, and stepped out for home. Benjy, on the end, reached out for Jonathon. More than anything he wanted to be locked in under those arms, but the solitary figure shuffling along Sidney Lanier Boulevard by the marsh stopped him.

"I'm going to wait for my folks," he said. Benjy raised a questioning eyebrow, hesitated and broke rank with the other two. Jonathon waved him off. Giving a half wave back, Benjy rejoined Craig and Alex as they walked away. When they were far enough along, and long before his parents came in sight, Jonathon, too, started trudging home.

Alone.

Chapter

11

Approaching home, Jonathon heard melodies from a pennywhistle. He didn't see anyone, but knew it was Sanders, in the tree. Avoiding the tree, he snuck by and into the house. In his kind heart he tried to tell himself he was giving Sanders privacy, but in his real heart he knew he had used up all the kindness he had for Sanders today. He wondered how many times a person's feelings could go up and down in one day without slinging right out of the body. Sanders was like the same wave repeatedly breaking over him.

Leaving a note for Mom and Dad, he slid his library book into his book bag, shook a "stay" finger at China and sneaked back out. The broad limbs of the tree shielded him as he twirled the combination of the lock, unlocked his bike and lifted it down the stairs. Without looking around, he pedaled off and when he was far enough down the street he breathed a "Whew."

This time he pedaled straight down Carr Street to the river and down River Street through Riverside Park. Smooth and unrippled from full high tide, the river reflected sky and clouds and seabirds as though they were flying through the river. A pelican floated, then met itself as it dove into the water, reality and reflection becoming one. Halfway submerging for a moment, the bird steadied itself, raised its beak and stretched its neck to swallow its catch. Jonathon scanned sky and water, wishing for sight of dolphin or even manatee. Once he had seen a manatee here, though Hanover was north of their usual range. Flat again, the water did not reveal so much as a ripple to show a pelican had just been fishing here. The sole action was in the skywater, where gulls, terns, cormorants flew without disturbing the water. Only at the peak of high tide or ebb of low was the surface of the water so glassy.

Finished with the river, Jonathon pedaled on to the library at the northern end of Riverside Park at the foot of Prince Street. He returned his book and browsed the shelves for another book to check out. When he stepped outside, he wondered how long it had taken since he'd left the house, for there was Sanders waiting by the bicycle rack. Had he stopped at the river for longer than he thought? How could Sanders be so fast? His first inclination was to duck back into the library but Sanders had already seen him and waved. Harder than being hateful in the first place, Jonathon realized, was being hateful after you'd been nice. Much as he didn't really want to be Sanders's friend, he wasn't going to do that to Sanders, or himself, again.

"You sure got down here fast," he said, smiling, at least acting friendly.

"I was waiting to ask you a question," Sanders said. "I was waiting at your house, in the tree, but you came and went so fast."

"I thought, uh, you wanted privacy."

"Well, yeah. That's what I thought you thought."

Jonathon secured the book bag over the handlebars, waiting for the question.

"You love music and I love music." Sanders

bobbed his head with pleasure at this love of music connection.

Still smiling, Jonathon mirrored the bobs. Of course it would be about music. What was he worried about? He hesitated to give Sanders a compliment, but Sanders deserved it. It was easy.

"You're really good, too."

"I know," Sanders said, grinning. "But thank you anyway."

Jonathon nodded with a flash of satisfaction at Sanders's confidence. He had confidence about his own music, too.

"You like books, too."

"Yeah?" Surely Sanders wasn't going to try to say he loved books, too. That would be too much.

"I hate books."

Ah, Jonathon thought, surprised at the truth.

"I, uh. Do you swear to secrecy?"

What now? Truth and fast turns. Did Sanders think it was a secret, this hating school, hating books? Jonathon sighed. Sanders made him sigh. He didn't remember going around sighing about things before Sanders. How did he keep getting in deeper with this boy when he didn't really want to be involved at all?

"Sanders, I don't really want your secret."

Sanders's eyebrows, eyes, mouth and chin rose in surprise, then drooped.

"But I want to tell you," he said eagerly. "I want to ask you something, but you have to swear to secrecy. I want you to do something for me."

Uh-oh, Jonathon thought.

"I want you to teach me how to read."

Jonathon was stunned speechless.

"Will you?"

Jonathon's mouth went dry from hanging open. Slowly, like the jerks of an inch worm, understanding crept into his skull and guts. All the horsing around in class was cover, cover for not knowing how to read. His hand drifted to his mouth to hold his astonishment inside. He'd heard about people who didn't know how to read, he'd heard about illiteracy. But he didn't know someone could be in school, be in sixth grade and not know how to read.

"Will you?" Sanders demanded.

Gravity seemed to be pulling his innards downward and turning them to stone.

"Well, er, um, uh." He had no idea what to say. "I don't know how to teach anyone to read," he said at last.

"Sure you do," Sanders insisted. "You read,

don't you? If you know how to do something, you know how to teach someone else."

Jonathon tried to reach back to first grade and learning to read. He remembered reading haltingly at first, baby words, then reading pretty well by the end of the year, but he didn't know how he'd learned. Now, it seemed he had always known how to read. He thought of Mom and Dad who seemed to know everything, and Dad might have time.

"Maybe my dad could teach you."

"No!" Sanders yelled in alarm. "You promised." He entwined his fingers and wrenched them back and forth.

Jonathon hadn't promised anything, but he could appreciate that if you'd made it to sixth grade hiding the fact that you couldn't read, then you wanted to keep it hidden. Still he was dumbfounded at the entire concept, Sanders unable to read and asking him for help. He struggled through his lack of knowledge and his unwillingness.

"How did you get to sixth grade if you don't know how to read?"

"I'm a good actor," Sanders said. "I manage."

"I sure know that. But how?" Jonathon pointed at the green street sign. "You mean you don't know what that says?"

"Streets are easy," Sanders said in a disgusted tone. "I know my way around. I know I'm at the corner of Prince and River streets."

"But you can't read the sign?"

"It says Prince and River."

"What about getting stuff at the store? What if you want a can of tomatoes?"

"It has a picture on it, stupid."

Jonathon felt puzzled and defeated.

"Streets and stores are easy. It's words in books, lots of words all together without pictures I can't figure out."

Jonathon's mind flashed back to the first day of school when Sanders refused to help hand out schedules. No wonder. He couldn't read the names. And in social studies when he'd been cutting up and reading the wrong things? He had been trying to "read" the pictures, spouting off about weapons when words beneath the pictures said tools.

"Will you teach me?"

The boy didn't give up. Jonathon rummaged through his head for an answer. "Maybe next summer," he said. "Maybe we can do it next summer."

Sanders hooted a sarcastic laugh. Summer, after all, was just now ending. "You're not going to help me."

Like a miracle, there was Mother driving up and calling out the window, "Want to go with me on the Saturday scrounge?"

"I, uh, yes," he said immediately. Usually he didn't enjoy going with her on her junk prowls and he marveled at her instinct for asking at just this moment.

"I, uh, well, I've got to go," he said to Sanders. She probably meant to park right here, since the flea market was just past the library down River Street, but he left his bike chained to its spot and leaped into the car. As Mom drove out of the library parking lot, he watched Sanders carefully, hoping he wouldn't catch on and follow. But the persistent boy stood unmoving as though he, too, were chained to his spot. Jonathon's internal stones began to rumble.

Mother darted him a questioning look, but didn't ask with words, and soon they were parked again and pushing between tables, browsing for what Mother saw as treasures. Jonathon tried to smooth himself by letting himself be captured by the array of stuff.

"Look at this." He lingered over belt buckles. There was every kind of design of every kind of thing designed into a belt buckle. Guns, animals, words, colors. "Look at this," he said to Mom as he looked and handled, "and this."

The buckle had such a nice heft. He thought they'd do better as paperweights than belt buckles. His middle was already heavy enough right now. "Maybe I'll start a belt buckle collection," he said to Mom before he realized she wasn't there.

Pretending he couldn't read, he wandered around to see what would be confusing but there was nothing to not understand. There was just pricing and a few signs such as "Belt Buckles" in front of the belt buckles.

Mother was standing over a table of dolls, not expensive antique dolls of which she had a few, but just someone's recently outgrown ones. She was holding, handling, the dolls, testing the cuddle, touching the cheeks and hair. Jonathon winced. Would this baby pain ever end? he wondered. For her or for him? And how about Dad? Did he have it too. As open as Dad was about so many things, he was guarded in what he said about the babies. And now Sanders had the baby pain. He'd never told Sanders he knew the feelings.

"You know?" she said and he scarcely heard her. His mind was drifting away, now, back to Sanders who loved music, who couldn't read, who tried to bluff his way along. "I can hardly bear the thought of those children not having dolls. What do you think about us buying them each one?"

"Huh?" They were at different angles on the same track. The George track. These tables, this crowd, this earth seemed to shift. He knew she would do it, knew they would be mixed up with Georges forever. He shoved his hands into his pockets and watched her examine the dolls.

"How many of them are there?"

"How should I know?" he said, even though he knew exactly how many. How come she didn't know herself? Had she walked past them all those times without really seeing? He guessed she had.

"Five girls," he told her. "Five girls in between two boys. The baby and Sanders, the boy I gave the pennywhistle to."

Mother busied herself about the selection. "I guess he'd be embarrassed to have a doll at his age," she said. "The older one."

"Yeah, I guess." He'd loved his dolls but yes, he too might be embarrassed to get one at this age.

"How's this?" Mother asked, six dolls in her arms, money out to the seller even as she asked Jonathon's opinion. "One for each of them and the one we already gave them can still be everybody's doll."

135

If they still have it, Jonathon thought.

The seller handed Mom a shopping bag and Mother put dolls in as tenderly as if they were alive. Immediately, turning from that table, Jonathon stopped so suddenly Mother bumped into him. For a moment he couldn't say a word. Down beyond the end of the roofed stalls was the yellow incubus and at the end table stood Mr. George.

"Would you look at that?" Jonathon said.

Mother looked.

For sale on Mr. George's table was the plastic three-wheeler and the doll Mother had given the girls.

Chapter

12

Poking her wrist through the handle of the shopping bag, Mother marched up to Mr. George's table and snatched up the three-wheeler and the doll.

He barked a protest but she barked back. "How dare you! How dare you! How dare you sell your children's toys!" Nearby, people looked over. He shut up and she stalked off. She sputtered and roared all the way home, and so did Jonathon's stomach.

From the bathroom he heard her telling Dad, still sputtering and roaring, and Jonathon knew he would try to teach Sanders to read. He didn't know how, but he'd find out. Maybe he could manage to ask Mom and Dad without giving away Sanders's secret. Tomorrow or Monday, he'd tell Sanders he would help. He now knew about the "young'uns" tearing things up. No wonder Sanders wanted to keep the pennywhistle in the tree.

All night his head and stomach stormed. Alex, Craig, Benjy, Sanders wouldn't stay out of his mind. Alex's "Who cares, anyway?" from their evening in Terra City, spun and spun. He cared. Sanders cared. They all cared, didn't they? Jonathon knew that whenever he himself said, "Who cares, anyway?" it was when he cared the most. Then why was he so isolated? Why were they all so isolated? They hadn't closed around him as friends, as they had always closed around one another. And he'd found it hard to be honest with them about Sanders. They'd lost something, though he didn't know exactly what, when he gave—or denied giving—the pennywhistle, or in the yard, when Craig buried and Alex stamped out Terra City. Dad said to think of what you can do, and he couldn't think of anything to do except that he could try to teach Sanders to read.

Milk might help his stirring stomach, he decided, so he padded barefooted from his bed and down the curved stairway. Trailing his hand along the railing he realized it was so smooth it seemed soft. For the first time he felt his mother's work in this banister, the way she'd sanded and varnished, sanded and varnished, sanded and varnished. There was comfort in this wood.

From out front, the streetlight shined through the leaded glass panels in angled patches. Crossing the hall he stepped only in the light, like rock-hopping a creek. When he opened the refrigerator door, a bright parallelogram spilled onto the floor and lit the kitchen dimly, almost like fog. He stood staring into the lighted box for a moment before he remembered what he'd come for.

Two o'clock, three o'clock, four o'clock, five. He saw the clock every hour of the night and heard the increasing bongs from the grandfather clock below in the entry. Toward morning, sleep still heavy in his eyes and the old grandfather clock just shy of bonging seven, he sat on the bottom stair rubbing one hand on China and one across the step. Mother even had the stair treads smooth as glass. He knocked on the wood, wondering how something that felt so soft could be so hard.

An echoing knock startled him. The shadow at the door made him jump. Hand on the newel post he swung himself up, looking at himself in pajamas. What would send someone to their door so early on a Sunday morning? He glanced up the stairs, expecting, wanting Mom or Dad to come shuffling from their bedroom.

Another hard knock.

Creeping to peek out the side panel, he saw Sanders standing there. In spite of his resolve to help Sanders learn to read, this felt like the incubus. Unlocking the door, he opened it just a crack.

"We're moving," Sanders announced.

Jonathon gave him a dumb stare. Who with good sense would wake someone up so early to say they were moving?

"We're *moving*," Sanders repeated in that brash voice that was so demanding.

"Uh, moving," Jonathon said, keeping the door only cracked to keep out the spirit of the incubus. There was a need to act normally, so he opened the door a standard measure. "Moving," he repeated, nodding to show he understood. "Where to?"

"Jacksonville."

"Jacksonville. Oh." This news surprised Jonathon awake. Jacksonville wasn't far, but it was out of town. Out of state even, seventy-five miles down the road into Florida. He'd thought Sanders meant somewhere here in Hanover.

Suddenly Sanders's face crumpled.

"Guess I won't never learn how to read."

It was as though Sanders was inside, behind the door, and had slammed it in Jonathon's face.

Now Jonathon slung the door open wide.

"Well, sure. Sure you will. I'm going to teach you. I was going to tell you. We'll start today. We'll practice a lot more before you leave."

Sanders gave the same snorting, hooting laugh he gave yesterday when he'd said, "You won't help me."

"You don't know anything, do you? We're *moving*," he said. "Right now. I'm not even supposed to be here."

"Now?" Jonathon peered out past Craig's house. The yellow incubus was backed into the yard almost to the porch steps.

"I got to go," Sanders said. "I told him I had to come tell you good-bye and he said don't leave the yard and I said I'm going, and I come. Thanks for being my friend."

"Wait!" Jonathon shouted. I haven't been your friend, he wanted to scream, but I want to. "Wait!" he said again and ran from the door and up the stairs with China leaping beside him. He ruffled quickly through the stacks of books on his bookshelf until he found some funny, easy books. China skittered beside him as he raced back down the stairs, afraid Sanders would be gone but there he was, waiting.

"Look, look," he said, waving the books, opening one.

China barked twice in her attempt to say, "Look, look!"

"These are easy and a lot of fun. Practice with them. You can read, I know you can. Ask someone else for help, you swear?"

"I can't."

"You can! You swear?"

"I swear." Sanders glanced down the street to where his father stood in the yard bellowing.

"You can have them," Jonathon said. "The books."

Sanders accepted. "Won't nobody get them. I won't let the young'uns tear them up. I swear." Jonathon didn't let on he knew what really happened to books and dolls and three-wheelers.

Sanders turned and ran to the tree, scrambling up and grabbing the pennywhistle from its secure place.

"I won't let anybody get this, neither," he said, waving the pennywhistle before he lifted

his T-shirt and tucked books and pennywhistle
into the top of his pants. He pulled the shirt
down over and ran down the street looking
pregnant. With books.

Jonathon darted to the music room for his
flute and in pajamas and, still barefooted, he
scampered into the tree, and China with him.
Setting the case carefully in a smaller niche in
the tree he put the flute together.

While he watched the reversal of what they'd
seen just a few weeks before, he played a flute
serenade. Furniture was dragged out of the
house to the porch. Heavy things were hoisted
by Sanders and his father. Small things were
carried by a parade of smaller Georges.

Benjy quietly appeared and perched in a nook
in the tree. Jonathon never ceased his playing.
Sanders showed no sign of hearing a note, but
Jonathon knew how far the music reached. Finally, the George parents climbed into driver
and passenger seat, Mrs. George no longer
pregnant but fat with George-George on her
lap. Various George children tucked themselves
into disappearance among furniture and mattresses and other belongings.

"I had things to talk with him about," Jonathon said. Music. And having babies die. China
whined as if she understood the whole sadness.

As the old bus drove away, Jonathon played a single note of flute music to trail the bus up George Street.

Among all the children, Sanders alone was visible.

He never looked back.